AT THE SIGN OF THE ROCKING HORSE

BY MARGARET POPE TRASK

Three for Treasure
At the Sign of the Rocking Horse

AT THE SIGN OF

The Rocking Horse

BY MARGARET POPE TRASK

Illustrated by Harold Berson

Thomas Y. Crowell Company   •   New York

AT THE SIGN OF THE ROCKING HORSE

CHAPTER 1.

CASSIE CLIFFORD sat in her tree house in the fork of the big maple tree. From her leafy perch she could see most of the village of Dublin Center, its white houses, its bright flowers and green vegetable gardens, its church steeple. She could see right into the window of Aunt Emerald's antique shop at one end of the big double house where Cassie lived. On another tree beside the road hung a wooden sign in the shape of a rocking horse. It was gaily painted, with a white-encircled eye, and on it was printed, "The Rocking Horse. Antiques. Emerald Blomquist, Prop."

Cassie was writing busily on a pad of paper in her lap. She heard a door slam across the road and saw Mr. Anson Fisher come out of the MacDougalls' house where he was boarding for the summer. He wore his wading boots, his canvas hat with a sun visor, and he carried a rod, a net, and a creel.

Cassie knew that he was on his way to the bridge down the road, the starting point for his daily activity. Mr. Fisher was a schoolteacher from New York, and Fergus MacDougall, who was Cassie's best friend, had told her that at night he wrote poetry; but every day he waded the stream, cast his line, and brought home such enormous quantities of trout that Fergus said they were plain sick of eating them.

It delighted Cassie and Fergus that his name was Mr. Fisher—Cassie thought he had probably taken up fishing just because of that. He was a small, thin man, formal and reserved, who had made few friends in the village—although several times he had come into the shop to talk to Aunt

Emerald about her antiques and had seemed quite friendly.

Cassie called to him from her platform. "Hi, Mr. Fisher! Are you going fishing?" She bubbled inside as she said it.

Mr. Fisher looked up and bowed seriously to her. "I am, indeed," he answered.

"Good luck," said Cassie, though for Fergus' sake she hoped he wouldn't catch anything.

"Thank you," said Mr. Fisher, bowing again, and he walked down the road with his precise stiff steps.

Cassie returned to her writing. Beside her was a half-empty bottle of Coca-Cola and a copy of the newspaper from the nearest city. It was folded to the announcement of a contest for schoolchildren. "SEE YOURSELF IN PRINT," it said. "Test your writing ability—you may have hidden talent! Write about anything of local interest, historical, geographical, human. Winning essay to be published weekly." Cassie had discovered the announcement yesterday and had at once decided to enter the contest.

She had been in the kitchen with her parents

when she found it. Her mother was rolling out a pie crust and her father was shelling peas for supper. Cassie was supposed to be helping him, but mostly she was reading the newspaper.

"Oh, boy," she said to him, "if only you'd had some good exciting adventure I could write about! A deputy sheriff ought to have lots of adventures and close calls and everything."

Her father smiled at her. "You look at too much television, Cassie," he said.

Cassie felt it was a terrible waste to have a father who was a deputy sheriff and yet had never made a single arrest, had not even had one run-in with a shady character. Dublin Center seemed to be a very well-behaved village; and Adam Clifford himself was the mildest of men, small and slight, with friendly eyes, not at all Cassie's idea of a lawman.

As well as being deputy sheriff he sold real estate, and was also game warden, tree warden, and selectman. Cassie was proud of everything he did, but the position of deputy sheriff was a great disappointment to her. The only calls her father received were like the one from Wilbur LaBarge the other day.

Cassie had answered the telephone and told Mr. LaBarge that he was not there.

"Well," roared the angry voice, "you tell him he's got to make Mert Bingham pay me fifty dollars for my vegetable garden. His cows got through the fence and et it all up."

No sooner had her father come home than Mert called. "Fifty dollars!" he shouted. "Why, all that little heifer ate was about four stalks of measly corn. You come over and see, before I flatten that guy."

So her father, sighing, had gone to the LaBarge farm, and when he came back he reported that he had considered the damage to the vegetable garden to be worth five dollars, which Mert Bingham had peaceably paid, and her father had noted that the fence was already mended. No one was flattened, and Mrs. LaBarge and Mrs. Bingham were rocking companionably on the front porch when he left.

"Haven't you ever done *anything* interesting?" Cassie asked him accusingly over the basket of peas.

"Well, I had to get one of Gramma Banks's kittens down from a tree for her the other day."

"Oh, *Dad!*" said Cassie.

"And I'm always on my guard that Mr. Anson Fisher doesn't catch over his limit of trout."

Cassie just looked at him. She said mournfully, "What *will* I write about?"

Her mother looked up from her pie crust. "Why don't you write about Aunt Emerald?" she suggested.

"Oh, Mom, I could, couldn't I? *She's* had plenty of adventures."

In her tree house, Cassie was already well into the essay on Aunt Emerald. She stopped writing and took a sip of warm Coca-Cola. In the back yard of the house next door Mrs. Hattie Banks's goat, Henry, was chewing up a cardboard carton. Cassie watched him absently and decided to read over what she had written. It was entitled "Success Story" and Cassie was pleased with it.

"In the village of Dublin Center," it began, "lives an amazing woman. She is my mother's aunt, so I know her well, and this is her story.

"About fifty years ago a girl by the name of Minnie Gates decided to run away from her home in Dublin Center and seek her fortune in New York

City. She was then nineteen years old, graceful as a deer and a beautiful dancer, but she knew it would break her old parents' hearts if she told them she was not satisfied with the simple life of a farmer's daughter in Dublin Center. So in the middle of the night she crept down the stairs with her suitcase, silent as an Indian, and walked the long miles to the nearest railroad station. She waited there till dawn when the train for New York came in, and boarded it for the great city.

"Arrived in New York, Minnie found a plain but clean room with a kind-hearted landlady in a boarding house. Of course she wrote her family right away and told them where she was and begged their forgiveness. She didn't have much money, so she got a job as a waitress in a restaurant. In her spare time she haunted the theatrical agencies and read all the notices of openings in choruses of musical shows. She also took dancing lessons with the money and tips she earned as a waitress. She decided she didn't have much chance of being a chorus girl with a name like Minnie Gates, so she changed it right away to Emerald Lamont.

"What was her good luck but to be chosen after a while to take the place of one of the girls who got sick in the chorus of the Ziegfeld Follies. She was in the back row but she didn't care. She wore a beautiful costume of red satin with tights and lots of spangles. It was while she was dancing in the Ziegfeld Follies that she met her future husband, Mr. Max Blomquist, a jeweler who was very rich."

Cassie sighed over what she had written, it was so romantic and so beautiful. She heard the bell over the door of the antique shop jingle and saw Aunt Emerald come out. She was wearing a large flowered straw hat, her pearl necklace and earrings, and was carrying a bushel basket.

Cassie leaned over the edge of the platform and called, "Aunt Emerald! I'm writing your story for the contest. Do you want to hear what I've written so far?"

Aunt Emerald looked up into the tree. Her white hair curled under the brim of her hat, and her tanned face was smooth, with only the wrinkles that laughter had given it. Her brown eyes smiled at Cassie.

"Yes, I'd like to very much," she answered.

"Come down and read it to me while I'm picking peas."

Cassie scrambled down the rope ladder with her pad under her arm and walked beside her great-aunt to the vegetable garden.

"I'm calling it 'Success Story,'" she told her. "Don't you think that's a good title?"

"Well," said Aunt Emerald thoughtfully, "I suppose you might call it that. But my life with Max always seemed so natural and so right that I never thought of it as anything spectacular."

"But all the jewelry he gave you! And traveling all over the world the way you did. Gee," insisted Cassie, "I think that was success after your humble beginnings in this little place."

Aunt Emerald laughed. "Read me what you've written," she said, and she put her basket down and leaned over the row of peas. Her emerald ring sparkled in the sun as she reached for the full pods.

Cassie began reading.

"Now wait a minute," Aunt Emerald interrupted almost immediately. "I didn't for a moment think it would break my parents' hearts. I just knew

my father wouldn't *let* me go to New York. He was a stern man and he had no sympathy with my dancing. I had to practice in secret in the barn. And I certainly was not as graceful as a deer."

"Oh, well," said Cassie, "it sounds better that way. That's what you call poetic license."

Aunt Emerald laughed again. "Have it your own way," she said.

Cassie finished reading and gave another sigh. "That's just the beginning. It's going to get even more exciting when I get to the part where you married him and went to India and Europe and everywhere to buy jewels for his business."

Aunt Emerald went on picking peas. She murmured, "Mm-m," and smiled under the shade of her big straw hat.

"Tell me more about how you met him," said Cassie. "Did he take you out to dinner and ply you with wine?"

"He took me out to dinner, but he did not ply me with wine. We went to a restaurant called The Witching Hour that had little lamps with pink shades on all the tables and there were gold birdcages with canaries that twittered and sang all evening."

"Did he ask you to marry him right away?"

"No," answered Aunt Emerald. "But I fell in love with him then and there and was scared to death that he wouldn't."

"Wasn't he a lot older than you?"

"Twelve years. But that made no difference to me. He was good and gentle and intelligent and humorous—what more could anyone ask?"

"So then what happened?"

"Well, he finally did get around to proposing, and of course I said yes, and we were married three days later."

"Didn't you want to come home and get married with your family all around you, in a white dress and flowing veil?"

"No," replied Aunt Emerald. "I really wasn't at all close to my parents. The only one I missed was my little sister, your grandmother."

Cassie was quiet for a minute. Then she said, "What I can't understand is what made you decide to come back here after Uncle Max died. My grandmother wasn't living any more—she died before I was born even."

Aunt Emerald stopped picking peas and looked at Cassie, half shaking her head. She said, "It was a very strange thing, really. I'd lived in New York for more than forty years and loved it, but suddenly it became the loneliest place in the world for me. I could have gone almost any place to live—we had good friends everywhere—but I didn't want any city without Max. I think my father's good New England farming blood came out in me then—I wanted country and green hills and a cow to milk. No one could have been more surprised than I was to discover I felt that way!"

"So you came right up here, didn't you, to look for a place to live? And lo and behold, the other half of our house was empty. Wasn't that *lucky!*" exclaimed Cassie.

"It was lucky for me," Aunt Emerald agreed.

"I'm going to write all about those little pink lamps and the canaries," Cassie said dreamily. "And then I'm going to tell about your travels in faraway places and all the jewels he gave you, particularly emeralds because of your name, and then I'll say that after he died you came back here because it was the only place in the world that seemed like home to you."

"You'll be just about right," remarked Aunt Emerald.

Cassie finished her composition that afternoon. The final paragraph read:

"So home at last in the Green Mountains of Vermont, Emerald Blomquist, wearing the priceless jewelry which reminds her of her beloved husband, runs her antique shop, tends her vegetable garden, and milks her cow. She is Dublin Center's most admired and loved citizen, not so much because of her jewels and her glamorous past, but because of her kind heart and her interest in everyone."

Cassie copied the essay neatly and put it in a large envelope. She addressed it to the office of the newspaper and put it in the mailbox under the Rocking Horse sign.

"Oh, I hope I win," she whispered. "I've just got to!"

CHAPTER 2.

AUNT EMERALD'S antique shop was the most delightful place Cassie knew. It was crowded with furniture, tables and highboys, desks and chairs, and on the walls hung clocks and brass warming pans and copper and iron molds. On every table and on the shelves of all the secretaries were pieces of old china, pewter plates and tankards, lamps that used to hold kerosene or whale oil, miniature bottles in the shape of rabbits or owls. On some of the chairs sat limp rag dolls, with faded, smiling faces.

There was more furniture on the front porch:

an old spinning wheel, a long settle painted black with dim gold fruit stenciled on its back, and a large rocking horse. He was white with black spots and he had a leather saddle with studs. His name was Mr. Gallup in honor of Homer Gallup who owned the grocery store.

Cassie had ridden miles on him when she was five years old and Aunt Emerald had come to live there and had started the antique shop. Almost the best thing of all about Mr. Gallup was that under his saddle was a little hinged door that lifted up to disclose a box-like compartment. Aunt Emerald thought that whoever had made him had cut out the door and put in the secret compartment as an added joy for a child; and Cassie had used it for years as a hiding place for her treasures. She was too old for that now, but she was not sure that there might not still be a gaudy ring won at a fair or a stale piece of gum in Mr. Gallup's dark inside.

Cassie helped Aunt Emerald keep the shop clean and dusted. She loved to flick the feather duster carefully over the delicate objects and the soft, mellow surfaces of the tables—it made her feel dainty and ladylike and old-fashioned. She pretended she was wearing pantalettes and a hoop skirt instead of blue jeans or shorts, and that her hair was fastened in a snood in back instead of hanging in two short pigtails, one on each side of her face. She talked to the dolls as she worked, giving them elegant names like Lady Lucinda or La Belle.

She had to stand on tiptoe to reach one of the clocks that stood on a shelf. It was her favorite thing in the whole shop. Aunt Emerald and Uncle Max had bought it long ago in Germany, and little carved figures used to revolve out of one doorway and into another whenever the hour struck. The clock no longer ran; its hands stood forever at four minutes past eleven, and motionless beneath its placid face Hansel and Gretel ran through the woods with the old witch just coming out of the doorway after them. Gretel's blue cape stood stiffly out behind her and under the dark trees a tiny rabbit and a spotted fawn watched them as they tried to escape. Cassie longed for the clock to run again and for the little figures to move, but Aunt Emerald said she didn't believe anyone could ever fix it.

The week after Cassie had mailed in her entry she was dusting in the antique stop, humming a song as she worked. Aunt Emerald had gone to an auction. Cassie was pretending she was the owner of the shop, although she knew her mother was just next door in case any customers came. The front door suddenly jangled furiously and in rushed Fergus MacDougall. Fergus, who lived across the road where Mr. Anson Fisher boarded, was a year older than Cassie, but they had been good friends since they were small. He was waving a newspaper over his head.

"Hey!" he shouted. "You've won! The paper's got your story all printed and it says you're the winner for this week!"

"Oh!" squealed Cassie, dropping the feather duster. "Did I really win? Let me see!"

"Here, right here," said Fergus, and he pointed to:

"Prize-winning Essay
SUCCESS STORY
by Ann Cassidy Clifford
Sixth Grade, Dublin Center School"

Underneath were the very words Cassie had written, the story of Aunt Emerald, marching neat and straight in small black print across the columns.

"Gee, isn't that *great!*" exclaimed Fergus.

Cassie couldn't even speak for a minute she was so overwhelmed at having won and at seeing her story actually printed in the newspaper. It looked so different, so formal and impressive.

Then she cried, "Oh, I've got to show it to Mom and Dad right away! Come on!" She grabbed the paper from Fergus and ran to the door at the end of the shop that led into their own kitchen.

Her mother was canning cherries and through the back door Cassie could see her father on a ladder picking more cherries from the big tree.

"Oh, Mom," she shouted, "I've won the contest!"

Fergus rushed to the back door and yelled, "Mr. Clifford! Cassie's won!"

Her mother said, "Oh, Cassie, how wonderful!" and she smiled all over her pretty round face. "I'm so proud of you! Oh, doesn't it look *nice?* Just imagine!" She hugged Cassie to her and Cassie squeezed her hard around the waist.

Adam Clifford came through the door, banging the screen behind him.

"What's this?" he said. "Is it really true?"

Cassie flew to him with the newspaper. "Look, it's right here—'Prize-winning essay, Success Story,' by *me!*"

"Why, Cassie, that's fine," exclaimed her father. He took the paper from her and spread it out on the table. They all leaned over it and stared at it in admiration.

"Aunt Emerald will be so pleased," her mother said. "We'll have a celebration over it at supper. I'll make a cake and decorate it saying, 'Congratulations, Cassie!'"

Cassie felt half embarrassed, half bursting with love for her family. "Oh, Mom!" she breathed.

Fergus clapped his hand to his forehead and rolled his eyes. "Yeeps!" he exclaimed. "I never thought I'd know a real author."

Aunt Emerald came home late that afternoon, her station wagon loaded with four pine chairs, a chest of drawers, seven hooked rugs, and a weather vane. Cassie rushed out to meet her with the newspaper, and Aunt Emerald sat right there to read it without even getting out of the driver's seat. She leaned out of the car and kissed Cassie.

"I'm flattered beyond words that you wanted to write about me, darling," she told her. "And I'm *so* proud of you for winning! You might even turn into a writer with that useful imagination of yours."

"Oh, I do want to be!" said Cassie.

The celebration at supper was very festive. Of course Aunt Emerald, who often had her meals in her own rooms over the antique shop, came to it, and Cassie invited Fergus, too. There were candles on the table and the best china and cloth napkins instead of paper. Cassie's father found a bottle of elderberry wine. Cassie and Fergus were each given a thimbleful and everyone took turns toasting Cassie.

Fergus became quite embarrassed and could only gulp and mutter, "Here's to ya," but Aunt Emerald raised her glass high, looked at Cassie with smiling eyes and said, "To my dear great-niece, the rising young author of Dublin Center." The elderberry wine might have been champagne, Cassie felt so bubbling inside. The beautifully decorated cake was delicious; Cassie ate two pieces and Fergus four.

"By the way, Aunt Emerald," Cassie's father said suddenly, reaching into his pocket. "Here's one of your earrings. I found it on the windowsill in the barn when I was milking Patience while you were away."

He handed her an emerald earring, brilliant green, sparkling in the candlelight.

"Thank you, Adam," said Aunt Emerald calmly. "I took it off when I was milking this morning. It seemed a little heavy."

Mrs. Clifford shook her head and clicked her tongue. "Aunt Emerald! You've *got* to be more careful of your jewelry. Leaving it in the barn, of all things!"

"I knew it was there, Annie," Aunt Emerald stated as though it were the most ordinary thing in the world. "I remembered it after I left for the auction."

Mrs. Clifford looked at her despairingly. "All day on the windowsill in the barn! Honestly, Aunt Emerald!"

"But what could have happened to it, dear? Patience wouldn't have eaten it."

"*Anyone* could have come in. Anyone could have found it and taken it."

"But who would want to do that?" inquired Aunt Emerald. "Who in this whole town doesn't know me and every bit of jewelry I have, and who wouldn't die rather than not return it to me?"

"But there *are* people we don't know," insisted Cassie's mother. "There's that queer Mr. Fisher at the MacDougalls', for instance. He might be a professional thief for all we know."

"Oh, Annie," laughed Aunt Emerald. "He's perfectly harmless—all he does is fish all day. And he's quite interested in antiques. We've had several good talks. In fact he wanted to buy Mr. Gallup, but I told him he wasn't for sale."

"Well, I don't know," said Cassie's mother. "And what about all the strangers passing through town who stop at the antique shop? We haven't any reason to trust *them*."

"They don't go to the barn, Annie," Aunt Emerald pointed out. "And when anyone comes into the shop there's always someone there, or at least near enough to hear the bell. And if none of us is around I *always* lock it up."

Mrs. Clifford sighed. "I think every bit of your jewelry should be in a safe-deposit box in the bank."

"Oh, Annie, what good would it do me there? Every time I put on a piece it reminds me of Max. I remember where we bought the stone, how he designed the setting—it gives me back my whole life with him."

"Well, if you just wouldn't be so careless about it," Mrs. Clifford scolded. "You treat it as though it came from the ten-cent store."

"Oh, no," Aunt Emerald objected. "I treat it as though it were simply a part of me. I can't wrap it in cotton wool and worry about it all the time. Max wouldn't want me to."

In the pause that followed they heard the screech of a car stopping suddenly outside; the front door banged and into the room clattered a young man with flaming red hair, wearing cowboy boots and a purple shirt. His name was Elmore Rivers, but he was called Red. He was the only son of the wid-

owed Mrs. Rivers, crippled with arthritis, and he had always been the town's bad boy.

When windows were broken or eggs stolen from chicken coops, it was Red who had done it; there were some who even thought he had been connected with the robbery of the gasoline station in Dublin Flats two years ago, although this was never proved. It was shortly after the robbery that Red had left town—to go West, he said; his mother grieved for him, but nobody else did.

"Hi, you all!" he shouted, beaming.

Cassie's father, in a voice that was not too friendly, said, "When did *you* get home? I thought you were out in the wild West."

"I was," said Red. "Just thought I'd come home and see Ma for a while—I'm on my way there now. Hi there, Fergus—Cassie. Gee, you've gotten real cute since I left." He gave one of her pigtails a tug and poked Fergus in the ribs. "Well, how's everything in little old Dublin Center?"

"It's all right," answered Cassie's father. "It's been very quiet and peaceful without you."

"Aw, now, Adam," roared Red, slapping him

on the shoulder. "Just you forget about those eggs I swiped and those deer I poached—I'm a reformed character now. How are you, Mrs. B.? You look wonderful! I haven't seen anything as pretty as those emeralds since I left."

"I'm very well, Red," said Aunt Emerald. "Your mother will be so glad to see you home. You behave yourself, now."

"Don't you worry, Mrs. B. Besides, I won't stay long enough to get in any trouble, this little town's too tame for me. I'm going to seek my fortune somewhere else, just the way you did once—hope I'll be as lucky as you were! Well, I'll be off now and surprise Ma. Be seein' ya." He gave them a jaunty salute and breezed out as noisily as he had come in.

"*Oh!*" exclaimed Mrs. Clifford. "That no-good! I wish he'd stayed away."

"I think he's good-looking," said Cassie.

Fergus frowned at her.

There was silence for a minute while Aunt Emerald absently twirled the ring on her finger. Then she leaned over and patted Mrs. Clifford's hand. "*Don't* worry, Annie, dear," she said. "He's wild and high-spirited, but there's no real harm in him. It was sweet of him to come back and see his mother."

"I suppose so," said Mrs. Clifford grudgingly. "But I just don't feel comfortable with him around."

Cassie felt that the mood of the party had become unnecessarily gloomy. She decided to bring the conversation back to her prize-winning essay. "Maybe I'll enter that contest again next week," she announced.

"What'll you write about?" asked Fergus.

"Well—" said Cassie, searching her mind, "—I could write about Batty Hattie."

"Cassie!" her mother admonished her. "You must *not* call her that."

"Oh, Mom, I know she's nice and kindhearted and everything, but she sure is batty."

Her father laughed. "Twenty-six cats and a lame crow," he murmured.

"And that smelly old goat," added Fergus.

Mrs. Hattie Banks, who was called Gramma by most of the village, lived next door to the Cliffords. Nobody knew how old she was, though some said it couldn't be less than ninety. She was shrunken but amazingly spry, with wispy hair tied with many little bows of gay ribbon, and pale blue eyes, as innocent as a kitten's. She always wore several gaudy-colored aprons, one on top of the other, and two or three brilliant scarves wrapped round her neck or fluttering from her wrist.

Colors were her delight: if she saw a bit of bright glass or broken crockery beside the road she stopped to pick it up, fondling it, turning it this way and that to glitter in the sun and then putting it in one of her many apron pockets to take home.

Her other love was animals. Stray or homeless, bedraggled or sick, Hattie Banks adopted them all. She fed them and cared for them, talking to them as though they were her children; there was always room for another in her tiny house. Hardly a week went by that a child did not appear on her doorstep carrying a basket from which could be heard high little mewings.

"Our cat had this litter of kittens," the child would explain, "and Ma says we gotta drowned them."

"Oh, the pore little things!" Gramma Banks would croon. "You set them right down inside here and I'll take care of them. Ain't they beautiful, now?"

Fergus said, "But I don't think you'd win any contest writing about Batty Hattie—I mean Gramma Banks. Most every village has got someone sort of crazy in it, but no one but us has got Mrs. Blomquist."

"Thank you, Fergus," said Aunt Emerald.

"Then maybe I won't write another after all," Cassie decided.

"That's right," agreed her father. "Give somebody else a chance."

"But if you had some good deputy sheriff adventure I'd write about *that.*"

"Don't worry," said her father. "I won't."

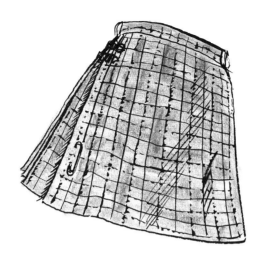

CHAPTER 3.

CASSIE had one day of glory after her composition was printed in the paper. People she met would say, "Good for you, Cassie—proud to know you." Homer Gallup, who ran the grocery store, gave her a free popsicle, and Gramma Banks insisted that she take one of her best pieces of broken glass, ruby red and quite large. Her schoolmates treated her with unaccustomed respect, and her teacher, who was spending the summer with her sister in Dublin Flats, called her up to congratulate her. Red Rivers took her for a wild ride in his white convertible. Her mother scolded her for going with him because he was such a reckless driver, but Cassie, windblown and flushed, thought it was the most glorious ride she had ever had. Fergus managed to be with her most of the time and acted as though he owned her. He made a point of telling the news to anyone who did not already know. "Hey," he'd announce, "what d'ya know? Cassie won the newspaper contest!"

Mr. Anson Fisher, acting unusually friendly and interested, brought her a glistening trout. Mrs. Clifford cooked it for supper, and Cassie, who was not so tired of fish as Fergus, ate it all herself.

But after one day everyone seemed to have forgotten the contest, and Cassie felt a little letdown. She spent a good deal of time in her tree house trying to write a mystery story. It was to be called *And the Door Creaked Closed.* The main character was an eleven-year-old girl who helped her father, the sheriff, capture a criminal who was trying to escape detection by pretending to be a ghost.

She was sitting there one day when Fergus appeared under the tree. He carried a brown-wrapped parcel.

"Hey," he said, "my Gram's sent me something more from Scotland."

"Oh, good," said Cassie. "I hope it's some more Edinburgh Rock."

Fergus' grandmother, who lived in Scotland, sometimes sent him presents—Scotch shortbread, or a necktie of tartan, or a little tuft of soft feathers held together by a silver band to wear in a hat. The last time it had been a box of taffylike candy called Edinburgh Rock, in assorted colors. You held it in your mouth and let it melt, tasting of nothing whatsoever but incredible, almost unbearable, sweetness. Fergus had never seen his grandmother, but she wrote him letters wishing he could come to Scotland and hoping that his father was teaching him to cast a trout fly properly and to do the Scottish dances.

"Dancing!" scoffed Fergus. "Sissy stuff."

Now he clambered up the rope ladder and sat down on the platform next to Cassie. He took a jack-knife from his blue-jeans pocket and cut the string of the package. He pulled off the paper and opened the box. Folded inside was some red and green woolen material cross-barred in blue. Fergus lifted it up and let it hang from his fingers. It was stitched in pleats, fringed at the slit that went up the front, and held together by a large safety pin.

"Yeeps," he said, "it's a skirt!"

"It's a kilt, you dope," Cassie told him. "Don't you know anything about what they wear in Scotland?"

Fergus said, "Yeeps," again. "Does she honestly think I'd wear this?"

"Oh, Fergus, it's beautiful! *Wear* it. You'd look so romantic in it."

Fergus' face turned red with embarrassment. "I'd rather die than wear a skirt," he muttered.

Cassie giggled. "I guess you would look sort of silly in it in Dublin Center. But *I* could wear it. May I, Fergus?"

"Take it," said Fergus, and he dropped it distastefully into her lap. Cassie put it on immediately, right over her shorts. It was much too large for her, so the waistband rested on her hips and the bottom edge hung far below her knees, but, delighted with

her costume, she spun and twirled and stamped her feet, while her pigtails bounced wildly.

"Look out," complained Fergus. "You'll bust the platform."

Just then a car drew up under the Rocking Horse sign. A round, bald man with a smooth face got out and started across the grass toward the door. He looked up and saw Cassie and Fergus in the tree and stopped.

"Good morning to you, birds," he said. His

voice was jovial and his smile made the corners of his eyes crinkle.

"Hi," responded Cassie and Fergus together.

"That's a nice place you've got up there. Tell me, do you know anyone around here who would rent me a room for a week or so? I've fallen in love with this little village and I'd like to stay for a while and do some painting."

"Are you an artist?" Cassie inquired.

"I like to think I am," answered the man, "though there are some who say I'm not." His eyes crinkled at them again.

Fergus said, "My mother takes boarders. We live just across the road."

"Has she got a free room?"

"Yes," replied Fergus. "We've only got one boarder now."

"His name's Mr. Fisher and he goes fishing all the time and he's also a poet," added Cassie.

"H'm, fine—then you're used to the artistic temperament. Who runs this antique shop?"

"My aunt does. Mrs. Blomquist."

"I'm crazy about antiques," observed the man.

"Well, I'll just trot across the road and see if your good mother will have me."

"I'll go with you," offered Fergus, and he lowered the ladder and climbed down.

In a few minutes he was back.

"He's going to stay," he told Cassie. "His name's Mr. Horace Bagley and he's a real nice guy, but, boy, you ought to see his paintings! Why, gee, I could draw better than that when I was in first grade."

"He's a modern, I guess," said Cassie, knowingly.

"Imagine selling that stuff. Boy, is it ever crazy!"

Cassie, and in fact the whole village, agreed with

Fergus as they came to know Mr. Bagley and saw what he painted. He set up his easel beside the road and daubed paint on the canvas in streaky lines and garish colors. The sides of the houses slanted, the roofs were askew, the grass was muddy yellow and the trees blue. Aunt Emerald's cow, Patience, appeared in one painting, but she was completely square, with legs like sticks and only one eye.

"It's symbolic, you know," Mr. Bagley pointed out, but no one asked him what he meant.

Cassie's father said, "You better not drink milk from that cow, Aunt Emerald. I don't think it's healthy."

But everyone liked Mr. Bagley. Unlike Mr. Anson Fisher he made friends with the old men who sat in the sun on Homer Gallup's porch, their chairs tilted against the wall. He brought Gramma Banks bouquets of bright field flowers and gave her a newly minted dime and two shiny pennies. Cassie was the only one who wasn't sure that she liked him. She felt that his painting had insulted Patience. "Besides," she said, "his eyes are too close together. They're like that man's who poisoned his brother on

TV to get his inheritance. I don't think he's trust-worthy."

"That's nonsense, Cassie," her mother reproved her. "A person can't help how his eyes are set."

Mr. Bagley spent almost as much time in the antique shop as he did painting. He had quite a knowledge of old furniture and endeared himself at once to Aunt Emerald by his extravagant praise of some of her pieces. He wandered about, picking things up, touching this and that, clicking his tongue in admiration. He bought a tortoise-shell snuffbox and a set of enamel buttons, though Cassie couldn't imagine what he wanted them for; and he also wanted to buy Mr. Gallup, but Aunt Emerald told him, as she had Mr. Anson Fisher, that he was not for sale.

Once when it was too rainy for Mr. Fisher to spend the day on the stream, he and Mr. Bagley were puttering around the shop together. Cassie thought they were an odd pair, Mr. Fisher so thin and reserved, Mr. Bagley so round and enthusiastic.

"Look at that now!" exclaimed Mr. Bagley, stopping in front of the clock with the little motionless figures of Hansel and Gretel and the witch. "Isn't that a rare thing?"

"It would be quite charming if it ran," Mr. Fisher commented in his stiff way.

"It doesn't though," said Cassie, afraid that one of them would buy it. "You can't make it run."

"Well, I don't know," mused Mr. Fisher. "There's an old Swiss watchmaker I know, I shouldn't be surprised if he could get it in order again. What would you sell it for, Mrs. Blomquist?"

"I wouldn't mind owning it myself," put in Mr. Bagley. "How about it, Mrs. Blomquist?"

"Oh," answered Aunt Emerald, "I'd have to think about that. It never occurred to me that anyone would want to buy it, since it doesn't run. I'm quite sure it can't be made to—the missing parts were handmade and nobody does that sort of thing any more. I wouldn't want to sell it to either of you on false pretenses."

Mr. Bagley laughed. "That's not the way to do business, Mrs. Blomquist!"

"Think it over," said Mr. Fisher. "Take your time."

"And while you're thinking," said Mr. Bagley coaxingly, *"do* reconsider about selling the rocking horse. It's such a delightful thing—I've never seen one with a hidden compartment before. I'd like to give it to a little boy I know."

Oh, *don't* sell Mr. Gallup, cried Cassie in her heart. She was relieved when Aunt Emerald said, "Oh, I don't believe I could let him go. I'll think about the clock."

"We can flip a coin to see which of us gets it, Anson," said Mr. Bagley.

Mr. Fisher remarked sourly, "It seems to me *I* was the first one who thought of buying it."

Mr. Bagley twinkled at him in a friendly way. "All's fair in love and war and antique-buying, Anson," he said.

Mr. Fisher said nothing, but Cassie thought he looked both determined and possessive as he stared at the clock.

CHAPTER 4.

THERE was a hand-lettered sign in Homer Gallup's window that said, "Turkey Supper, St. Thomas' Church, July 20th, from 5:30 until all are served. Braided rug and pig raffle. Bingo. Pony rides. Jessup's Midget Marimba Band."

Almost everyone was helping to get ready for it. Booths were built on the green beside the church and wires strung between trees for the colored lights and pennants. The Cliffords' kitchen was spicy with the smell of pies Cassie's mother was

44

baking for the food sale. Even Cassie had promised to contribute four dozen brownies.

"Buy some of them back, Mom," she begged. "I make such good brownies I don't want other people to get them all."

"Don't be conceited, Cassie," said her mother.

"Or greedy," added her father, winking at her.

Mrs. Gallup had been working all winter on the braided rug that was to be raffled, and the pig was to be supplied by Mert Bingham. Cassie thought the rug was beautiful: it was red and blue, and nine feet long. She hoped her mother would win it. Fergus had bought a chance on the pig, but he was saving most of his money for the games. Mr. Bagley offered to donate one of his smaller paintings as a prize for bingo, but the committee tactfully refused it.

All day on the twentieth there was activity at the church. Hammers pounded and men shouted and joked. In the big basement room the women set up rows of tables and benches for the supper, and in the kitchen they made enormous bowls of potato salad, and heaped platters with rolls and biscuits and pickles and jellies, and filled the huge coffee maker. Cassie made two trips to the baked goods booth to deliver the pies and brownies, and she helped blow up the balloons that Fergus and Red Rivers thumbtacked to the back of one of the booths for dart throwing.

"I'll treat you to a game tonight, Cassie," said Red. "Bet you'll bust 'em all, you'll be so good."

In the afternoon Mr. Tobin from Dublin Flats arrived with the ponies and staked out the riding ring. There were seven Shetland ponies with flowing manes and tails, and a little colt. It was cream-colored and fuzzy, with a stubby mane that stood up like a scrubbing brush, and dark, wide-apart eyes. It stood staunchly on its straight little legs with their tiny polished hooves, and the tips of its pointed ears were no higher than Cassie's waist. She knelt in front of it and put her arms around its neck.

"Oh, what's his name?" she asked Mr. Tobin.

"Ain't got none yet. I ain't had time to set my mind to it, I been so busy lately. Want to name him?"

"Oh, *yes!*" said Cassie. She sat back on her heels

and thought hard. The colt nuzzled against her shoulder and rubbed its nose, as soft as peach skin, against her cheek. Suddenly it jumped away, arched its neck, and bounced straight up in the air, coming down on all four legs as stiff as a kitten. Cassie laughed aloud. The colt shook its head saucily, flicked its short tail, and made a high-pitched noise, half snort, half squeal.

"He's no bigger than a minute," said Cassie tenderly. "Oh, why don't we call him that—Minute?"

"That'd do fine," said Mr. Tobin.

"Thank you for letting me name him." Cassie kissed the colt on its forehead. "Good-bye, Minute darling. I'll come back and see you lots tonight." She ran home to get ready for the supper. As she crossed the bridge she could see Mr. Anson Fisher far up the stream. He's *still* fishing, thought Cassie—he must be crazy!

Mr. Bagley was sitting on a camp chair beside the road painting a picture of the antique shop. Cassie said to him, "Aren't you coming to the church supper, Mr. Bagley?"

"Yes, of course. But I do want to take advantage

of this late afternoon light and just finish this up. The shadows are very interesting."

Cassie looked thoughtfully at the painting. She thought it was the worst he had yet done. "The steps are sort of falling down, aren't they?"

"That's to arouse the feeling of antiquity in the beholder," explained Mr. Bagley.

"Oh," said Cassie.

She went in the house and changed into her yellow and white flowered skirt and shook all the money she could out of her piggy bank. There was seventy-three cents. Cassie put fifty cents in her pocket and dropped the rest back into the pig. "I don't want to spend it *all* at the fiesta," she said, feeling virtuous and thrifty.

"Hurry up, Cassie," called her father. "Everyone's gone."

Her parents and Aunt Emerald were waiting for her as she ran downstairs. Aunt Emerald was wearing a red printed dress, a ruby necklace, and a ruby ring.

"Oo-oo," said Cassie. "You look beautiful, Aunt Emerald!"

"I decided to be flamboyant all in red," Aunt Emerald told her.

"Have you locked up the shop?" asked Cassie's mother.

"Certainly," replied Aunt Emerald rather haughtily. "You have got to stop worrying, Annie."

Mr. Bagley waved a paintbrush at them as they started down the road. "Save me a seat," he called.

Gramma Banks was puttering in the garden beyond her house. "Don't you want to come with us, Gramma?" called Cassie's mother.

"I'll be along later," she said. "I ain't comin' to the supper—can't eat that hearty food—but I'll get there in time for the raffles."

At the steps of the church Mrs. Gallup sat at a card table selling final chances on the braided rug that hung from the branch of a tree. Beside it, in a makeshift pen, the pig snuffled and pushed at its dinner of lettuce. Cassie leaned over to pat its prickly back. "Nice pig," she said.

The basement room was crowded with people standing in line to be served or already eating at the long tables. Cassie loaded her plate with turkey and cranberry sauce and several kinds of salad, and ate as fast as she could. Mr. Bagley arrived just as she was finishing her chocolate pie and she gave him her place at the table and rushed outside. On a platform the marimba band had begun to play, directed jerkily by Mr. Jessup himself. The band was made up entirely of children. Cassie thought it would be wonderful to play in a children's band and wear a green and white uniform. She said so to Fergus whom she found there, watching and listening.

"Naw," said Fergus. "You'd have to practice all the time. Come on, let's get going."

They went from one booth to another. Fergus won two paper leis for puncturing balloons with darts and a small plaster Scottie dog for throwing baseballs into milk cans. They checked up at the food counter and found that all Cassie's brownies had been sold. At the soft-drink booth they met Mr. Anson Fisher, who informed them that he had just arrived and hoped they were enjoying themselves. "I was sorry to miss the supper," he said, "but I got in too late from fishing."

They each drank a bottle of orange pop and Fergus ate a hot dog with mustard and pickle relish.

"How *can* you?" said Cassie. "You've just finished supper."

"I've got a growing boy's appetite," explained Fergus.

"You're disgusting," said Cassie. "Come see the baby pony."

At the pony ring small children with very serious expressions were going round and round on the backs of the short-stepping ponies, jolting up and down, clutching the pommels. The colt, Minute, lay with his front legs bent under him. His eyelids were lowered and his straight blond lashes stuck out in a thick fringe.

"Aw, he's cute," whispered Fergus.

Cassie knelt beside him. He woke up at once and gave his little whickering squeal. Cassie plucked a handful of grass and held it out to him. He munched it eagerly, tickling her with his soft lips, breathing warmly on her hand.

"Isn't he *darling?*" she said.

There was the sudden noise of a speeding car down the road and they looked up, startled. The dust flew under the wheels of Red Rivers' white convertible as he went tearing past them. His hair seemed more fiery than ever, and his mouth was set and strained-looking. He roared by without a glance at anyone and was gone in an instant.

"Gee," said Fergus. "He's sure in a hurry."

Mr. Tobin shook his head. "That boy's going to come to no good, mark my words."

"I wonder where he's going," said Cassie, aggrieved. "He told me he'd treat me to dart throwing."

"Out of sight, out of mind," said Mr. Tobin. "I coulda told you he wasn't reliable."

Cassie was sorry Red Rivers hadn't come to the fiesta, but she soon forgot him. She and Fergus stayed with Minute for a while longer, stroking him and feeding him grass, and then they went back to the booths. Fergus bought another hot dog and Cassie bought a surprise package at the grab bags. It contained a knife with a rubber blade, a sheriff's tin star, and a tiny tea set inside a wooden apple. She immediately went in search of her father, whom she found at a table playing bingo with Aunt Emerald and Mr. Fisher, and gave him the medal.

"Thanks," he said. "Now maybe people will respect me more," and he pinned it to his shirt pocket.

It was dusk by now and the orange lights strung between the trees were turned on. They made everything look theatrical and exciting. The bright-colored pennants waved in the gentle breeze. The crowd moved contentedly about, dogs wandered here and there, babies were given bottles on the church steps, the marimbas clinked and trilled. One of Gramma Banks's cats sauntered down the road and jumped into an empty baby carriage where it tucked its front feet together and went to sleep, purring loudly.

"Oh, I *love* fiestas!" sighed Cassie.

"I'm getting tired," said Aunt Emerald. "I wish they'd have the drawing on the rug and then I'd go home."

At that moment Mert Bingham mounted the church steps carrying a cardboard carton. The band beat a rat-a-tat-tat on the marimbas and Mert announced loudly, "Now, folks, gather round for the raffles. First we'll have the pig and then the rug.

That pig's going to make mighty fine eating. Emerald Blomquist, you come up here and do the drawing."

Aunt Emerald stood up, smiling. "Oh, Emerald's wearing her rubies!" remarked a delighted voice from the crowd. Other voices called to her, "Remember he's got my number on him, Emerald," "I'll ask you to a ham dinner if you pick mine!"

Fergus pleaded, "Please draw sixty-one, Mrs. Blomquist. That's my number and ham's my favorite food."

Aunt Emerald made her way through the crowd and stood on the steps beside Mert. Her necklace sparked and glinted under the lights, and her ring flashed as she reached her hand into the carton. She drew out a slip of paper and handed it to Mert. He pushed his spectacles back and unfolded the paper.

"Number ninety-three," he called out. "NINE THREE! Who's got it?"

A little fluttery voice near them cried, "I've got it! I've got ninety-three!" Gramma Banks, with six pink ribbons in her hair, moved toward the steps.

"Congratulations, Gramma," said Mert. "You're sure going to enjoy eating that pig. I corn-fed him myself."

"Eating him!" quavered Gramma Banks. "Why, that lovely pig, I wouldn't any more *eat* him!" She went straight to the pen where the pig stood. "Now, dearie, you're coming to live with Gramma," she crooned. The pig looked solemnly at her with its little pink eyes. Gramma Banks leaned over and scratched it behind the ears. The pig closed its eyes and snuffled contentedly.

"That'll make twenty-nine animals living next door," Cassie's father grumbled.

"Oh, well," remarked her mother resignedly. "She loves them so."

"I think it's a *nice* pig," declared Cassie.

Mert Bingham had brought another carton out from the church. He raised his hand. "Quiet now!" he called. "We're going to have the drawing on this beautiful braided rug, which we're all very grateful to Clara Gallup for making. I know we'd all be real proud to own it. Draw again, Emerald. Let's see who's lucky this time."

"Oh, I know you're going to win it, Mom—thirteen's your lucky number!" said Cassie, jumping up and down. "Let me hold the ticket." She clutched it tightly and held her breath.

Aunt Emerald put her hand into the carton and with a flourish pulled out another slip of paper. Mert opened it and read dramatically, "Number *one—twenty—four!*"

Cassie let out her breath and crumpled up the ticket.

"Never mind, Cassie," her mother consoled her. "We've got plenty of rugs—I don't know where I'd put it. Who's won it?"

They all looked around. From the back of the crowd came Mr. Bagley, waving a ticket over his head, beaming with smiles.

"Oh, that old Mr. Bagley," Cassie muttered crossly. "What's *he* going to do with it?"

"Cassie," said her mother severely, "you have got to stop being so unreasonable about Mr. Bagley. He may paint silly pictures, but he's a nice man and he makes himself very agreeable to everyone."

Mrs. Gallup gathered up the rug in her arms and

came forward to meet him. "I'm proud to have an artist own it," she told him with a twinkle in her eyes. The crowd laughed and Mr. Bagley bowed to all sides and shook hands with himself above his head.

Aunt Emerald came down the steps to the Cliffords. "This old lady's had enough. I'm leaving."

"Let me see you home," said Mr. Anson Fisher.

"No, no," said Aunt Emerald. "There's no need for that."

"Well, I believe I'll be going anyway—I've had a long day on the stream. So I'll escort you."

"We'll be along soon," promised Mrs. Clifford.

"Don't hurry," said Aunt Emerald, and she and Mr. Fisher started down the dark road with their flashlights.

The band burst into a final clatter of noise. The youngest marimba player yawned widely and drooped over his instrument. Parents began to collect their children, and small voices cried passionately, "Oh, Ma, not *yet!*" Cassie spent her last dime on a hot dog and went once more to see Minute. She gave him the end of her bun, which he ate with enthusiasm. Reluctantly she kissed him good-bye.

Cassie's father offered to help Gramma Banks drive her pig home. He was just getting ready to let it out of the pen when they heard Aunt Emerald's voice calling, "Adam! Annie!"

She was coming back down the road, half running, stumbling. She looked changed—suddenly smaller and older—and Cassie's stomach went abruptly hollow with the fear that something dreadful had happened.

"What is it, dear?" cried Mrs. Clifford, and Cassie echoed, "Oh, what's the *matter,* Aunt Emerald?"

Aunt Emerald looked at them with stricken eyes. She took a breath and let it out on a quivering sigh.

"It's gone," she said. "All my jewelry's gone."

They looked at her as though her words made no sense. Cassie's father said roughly, "What do you mean?"

"It isn't there any more. My jewelry box is empty." Aunt Emerald spoke in a dead voice. Her face was white.

"Oh," cried Mrs. Clifford, "it's been stolen! I *told* you it would be!"

"Maybe you just mislaid it," Cassie's father said. "Did you look everywhere?"

"Where could I look?" said Aunt Emerald. "Where could it be except where I left it, on my own bureau in my jewelry box?"

It was so dreadful and Aunt Emerald looked so hopeless, so empty and old, that Cassie could not bear it. She began to cry.

"But how did anyone get in?" barked Cassie's father. "You locked the door before we left."

"I don't know," said Aunt Emerald in her tired broken voice.

"Oh, Aunt *Emerald!*" sobbed Cassie.

People had gathered close around. They looked at each other with unbelieving faces and spoke in horrified voices. "Emerald's jewelry's been stolen!" "Stolen!—no—who would have done that?"

Cassie's father spoke loudly and wrathfully. "Now look here—has someone been . playing a joke?"

No one answered, but there was a shocked intake of breath. Then Mr. MacDougall, Fergus' father, roared, "That wouldn't be no joke. No one here'd play that kind of dirty trick on Emerald!"

"Adam, what are you going to do?" Mrs. Clifford cried frantically. "You've got to *do* something!"

"I'm going to do something," said Cassie's father harshly. "I'm going back and check the house and then I'm going to call the State Police."

He went down the road at a run.

CHAPTER 5.

IT seemed as though the whole village streamed after him. Aunt Emerald walked slowly, her arm in Mrs. Clifford's, and Cassie held tightly to her other hand.

"It'll be all right, Aunt Emerald," she kept repeating through her sniffles. "Dad'll find it, I know he will." It *must* have been a joke, she thought —someone had hidden it. But the summer night felt unfriendly and scary in spite of the little golden pools from the flashlights.

The windows of The Rocking Horse and of the rooms above it were all alight when they got there. Cassie's father was just coming out the front door of the antique shop. He came straight to Aunt Emerald.

"The side window of the shop's been forced open," he told her. "I've called the police. Corporal Phelps will be right out."

Cassie's heart sank. Then someone *had* broken in and it was horribly true—all Aunt Emerald's jewelry had been stolen.

Fergus, behind her, called breathlessly, "It was Red Rivers, Mr. Clifford! He drove out of town while we were at the fiesta and he was going like crazy."

"What! I didn't see him."

"He did, didn't he, Cassie? And he looked awful funny."

Cassie remembered the look on Red Rivers' face and the breakneck speed of his noisy car. He must have done it, she thought—and felt angry and betrayed because she had liked him in spite of his wild ways.

But Aunt Emerald said, "Oh, no, Adam, I don't think he did it."

"I shouldn't be surprised," said Cassie's father, his face dark. "Who else?"

At that moment Mr. Anson Fisher stepped out of the MacDougalls' door. He looked around at the crowd of people with a surprised expression.

"Is something the matter?" he asked, coming across the road.

"Plenty," replied Cassie's father. "All Mrs. Blomquist's jewelry's been stolen."

"Stolen!" exclaimed Mr. Fisher. "How shocking! When did it happen?"

"While we were all down at the church." Adam Clifford looked sharply at Mr. Fisher. "By the way, you didn't come to the supper, did you? What were you doing all the time?"

Mr. Fisher drew himself up. "I was fishing until quite late," he said. "After I'd cleaned my fish it was nearly seven o'clock and I thought they'd be through serving by then. So I simply ate a sandwich left over from my lunch and came along to the festivities. Furthermore, Mrs. Banks was sitting on her front porch when I came back and she was still there when I left. She saw me both times." He smiled coldly.

"Okay," said Cassie's father. "I better call in the description of Red's car right away. Does anyone know his license number?"

No one spoke and Cassie's father swore under his breath. He went quickly into the house.

"You come inside, too, dear," Mrs. Clifford said to Aunt Emerald. "I'm going to make you a cup of tea."

Cassie and Fergus were left standing by the road with Mr. Fisher, who looked huffy. Mr. Bagley came up to them. His usually smooth forehead, which went right up into his bald head, was furrowed.

"This is a terrible thing, Anson," he said. "Who would do that to Mrs. Blomquist?"

"It was that Rivers boy, of course," said Mr. Fisher. "I understand he has a very bad reputation."

"Yes, it must have been." Mr. Bagley shook his head and clicked his tongue. Then he frowned. "And yet Mrs. Blomquist didn't seem to think he'd done it. That's odd."

"I don't think he did, either," said Cassie, her loyalty reasserting itself.

Mr. Fisher said nothing. Mr. Bagley continued to frown and to look thoughtfully at him.

"Anson," he said after a moment, "suppose he did have some other reason to leave town suddenly —you know what position that leaves us in?"

"What do you mean?" asked Mr. Fisher.

"You know how everyone feels about Mrs. Blomquist—the whole town loves her and they all take a personal pride in her jewels. Now, we're the only strangers here. One of *us* is going to be suspected."

"Well, I don't know about you," said Mr. Fisher irritably, "but *I've* got a perfectly good alibi. Mrs. Banks saw me come back from fishing and she saw me leave for the church. She was sitting on her front porch all the time."

"I'm afraid that's not going to do you much good, Anson—Batty Hattie, as these children call her, isn't a very reliable witness. No, these good people are all going to assume it was one of us."

"Nonsense!" Mr. Fisher spat out.

"It's true," said Mr. Bagley, keeping his eyes fixed on Mr. Fisher's face. "But I tell you what we can do, Anson. We can voluntarily ask for a search of our rooms."

Slowly Mr. Fisher's face turned dark red.

"You wouldn't want to?" inquired Mr. Bagley softly.

Mr. Fisher made sputtering noises like a damp firecracker.

"I imagine the police will do it automatically when they get here," Mr. Bagley went on in his gentle voice. "Don't you think it would be a good idea to suggest it ourselves?"

"Well," Mr. Fisher exploded. "There certainly isn't anything I want to *hide.*"

"Fine!" exclaimed Mr. Bagley. He took him firmly by the arm and led him straight to Cassie's father, who had just come out of the house. Cassie and Fergus stared at each other.

Mr. Bagley spoke to Adam Clifford. "We feel *terrible* about this, Anson and I. Particularly as we're the only strangers here, the only ones who aren't old friends of Mrs. Blomquist, and we think you might quite naturally feel suspicious about us. We'd both appreciate it if you'd make a thorough search of our rooms right away."

Cassie's father looked surprised. Mr. Bagley went on earnestly, "We want to prove to everyone that we had nothing to do with this shocking theft. Isn't that right, Anson?" He still held Mr. Fisher by the arm.

Mr. Fisher cleared his throat. "Yes," he said, without enthusiasm.

Cassie's father looked at first one and then the other. "All right, I will," he declared. "It'll give me something to do until the police get here." He turned to Fergus' father. "Andrew, you go get Mrs. Rivers—they'll want to talk to her. Come on, you two."

"Can we watch you search?" asked Cassie in excitement.

"No," said her father emphatically. He led the way to the MacDougalls' house, followed by Mr. Bagley and Mr. Fisher. Cassie and Fergus, disappointed, trailed across the grass and sat down on the steps of the antique shop. Behind them the spinning wheel loomed in the shadows and Mr. Gallup stood, noble and still. Cassie leaned back and patted his nose, and he began to teeter quietly on his rockers.

Fergus said in a low voice, "Mr. Bagley thinks Mr. Fisher stole it."

"I bet he did. I *knew* it wasn't Red Rivers."

"I bet it was."

"It was not," said Cassie. "If it wasn't Mr. Fisher, it was Mr. Bagley. I never did trust him—his eyes are too close together."

Fergus scratched his head and thought. "It couldn't have been," he said at last. "Why would he stick around and let your father find it in his room? He *couldn't* have hidden it so well he wouldn't find it."

"Maybe he buried it."

"He didn't have time to, not and completely disguise the place the way he'd have to—he came to the supper just a little while after you did. And I don't see how Mr. Fisher could have stolen it at all. He wouldn't have dared go over and break in with Gramma Banks sitting on her front porch all the while."

"But Mr. Bagley said the police wouldn't believe her," Cassie reminded him.

At just that moment Gramma Banks herself came into sight on the dim road, accompanied by the pig. Occasionally she poked it gently with a stick, but mostly it walked beside her, docile as a dog. Cassie and Fergus watched their progress. They could hear the pig snuffling in an adenoidal way, and as she pushed it lovingly into the yard they heard Gramma say in her high, thin voice, "Here's where we live, dearie."

A sudden appalling thought came to Cassie. She knew from the way Fergus looked at her that he must have had the same thought at the same minute. "Fergus!" she whispered. "*She* was the last person to come to the fiesta. Oh, do you think it was *her?*"

Fergus nodded slowly. "I bet," he whispered back. "Look how she likes bright-colored things."

"But could she have broken in the window?" Cassie asked. "She's so little."

"Yes, but she's strong and awful spry," Fergus pointed out. "I bet you anything she did. I knew it couldn't have been Mr. Bagley or Mr. Fisher."

Cassie tried to think of Gramma Banks climbing in the window of the antique shop, tiptoeing up the stairs, scooping up the glittering necklaces, the bright rings and bracelets and earrings. It was just the sort of crazy thing she would do; they would be a thousand times better than her pitiful pieces of broken glass.

"But Fergus!" she exclaimed suddenly. "If she took them she's probably got them right out in plain sight in her house. She wouldn't want to sell them or anything, she'd just want to *look* at them."

"That's right," Fergus agreed.

"We ought to tell Dad!" Cassie cried.

"Let's look ourselves," said Fergus, jumping up. "She'll let us go in. We can say we want to see the kittens."

They ran next door. Gramma Banks had opened the gate of the small enclosed yard where Henry, the goat, lived and was pushing the pig inside with friendly pats. "This is Henry, dearie," she said. "Henry, I want you to meet my pig." Henry looked with baleful yellow eyes at the pig and wiggled his beard.

"Mrs. Banks, could we go in and see the kittens?" Fergus asked.

"Of course you could. They'll be so happy to see you!" Gramma Banks beamed at them.

The kitchen was dark and filled with the warm throaty noise of purring. Fergus snapped on the light and they saw cats of all sizes, curled on the chairs, sitting on the table, cuddled in soft heaps in boxes and cartons. The lame crow flew squawking from the top of the stove to peck at Fergus' shoe-laces. A small yellow kitten danced sideways toward Cassie; she couldn't resist picking it up to hold against her cheek. It purred in her ear like a tiny electric motor.

Fergus nudged the crow away from his shoe. "Come on," he said. "There's nothing in here."

It was unbelievably cluttered in the living room. There were quantities of wobbly wicker furniture, all painted red or yellow or green, and an ancient player piano draped in a Paisley shawl. The sofa was covered with a ragged but gaudy patchwork quilt. On tables and shelves, on the top of the Franklin stove, were chipped ornaments, bits of shiny metal, stones that sparkled, and cracked glass that shone. From every lampshade hung cheap strings of bright beads.

But there was no valuable jewelry anywhere. Cassie and Fergus investigated the living room and the bedroom, weaving their way around the dilapidated furniture. Fergus looked under the bed and peered through the drafts of the Franklin stove.

"But she wouldn't *hide* it," Cassie insisted. "I know she wouldn't. She'd leave it right out where she could look at it all the time."

"I guess she would," Fergus admitted. "But, gee, I thought sure we'd find it here."

"So did I," said Cassie. "Oh, poor Aunt Emerald, all her beautiful jewelry gone! Oh, I *hope* they found it in Mr. Bagley's or Mr. Fisher's room. Maybe they have!"

They rushed outdoors. Mr. Fisher, more expansive than usual, was talking to a group of people while Mr. Bagley stood silently by. Cassie thought he looked disappointed. Down the road came Fergus' father; beside him, agitated and red-eyed, limped Red Rivers' mother.

Cassie ran to her father. "Didn't you find anything, Dad?"

He shook his head.

"Did you rip open the mattresses?" cried Cassie.

"No," said her father crossly. "I wish Corporal Phelps would hurry up and come."

He had hardly spoken when a sharp needle of light appeared far down the road and they heard the whine of a siren. With its searchlight blazing and its tires squealing, the police car drew up in front of The Rocking Horse.

Chapter 6.

CORPORAL PHELPS wore a gray flannel suit and smoked a pipe. He looked young and not at all like a detective, Cassie thought. With him was Trooper Wallace, an immense man, heavy jowled, who wore his uniform as if it grew on him. His brass buttons shone, his wide belt flowed smoothly around his middle, and a pistol gleamed coldly from the holster at his side. Fergus simply opened his mouth and stared when he saw him: Trooper Wallace was everything you expected of the law.

Cassie's father met them as they got out of the car. "I'm sure glad you're here, Corporal," he said. "Where do you want to begin?"

"I'll talk to Mrs. Blomquist first," answered Corporal Phelps, tapping out his pipe on the heel of his shoe.

Red Rivers' mother hobbled forward and seized him by the arm. "Oh, mister," she said vehemently, "my boy didn't steal it. I know he didn't."

Cassie's father said, "This is Mrs. Rivers, Corporal. Her son left town in a hurry this evening. I've called in a description of him and his car."

"Why did your son leave so suddenly, Mrs. Rivers?" asked the corporal.

Mrs. Rivers brushed at her eyes with her gnarled old hand. "We'd had a mite of an argument. He's hot-tempered, you know."

"What was the argument about?"

Mrs. Rivers hesitated. "Well—it mighta been about money. But he didn't steal nothin'. I just *know* he didn't."

The corporal turned to Trooper Wallace. "You get a statement from Mrs. Rivers, Willie, while I see Mrs. Blomquist. And do something about getting rid of this crowd—they're no help."

"Yes, sir," said Wallace in a deep growl. He took Mrs. Rivers by the arm. "Now, ma'am, we'll find a nice comfortable place to sit and you can tell me all about it."

Cassie followed her father and the corporal into the house, leaving Fergus to gaze in awe at Trooper Wallace. Aunt Emerald was sitting on the couch in the living room beside Mrs. Clifford. Cassie was glad to see that she looked better, though still pale.

"Here's Corporal Phelps," said Adam Clifford. "This is Mrs. Blomquist, Corporal, and this is my wife."

Corporal Phelps nodded and drew up a chair. "I'm very sorry to hear about this, Mrs. Blomquist," he said. "Tell me what you can, will you?"

Cassie's mother burst out, "I always told her she shouldn't keep that valuable jewelry around, Corporal."

Adam put his hand on her shoulder. "Hush, Annie. Let Aunt Emerald talk."

"There's not much I can tell you," Aunt Emerald began. "It was all the jewelry my husband had given me, a great deal of it. I've had it for a long time, and it was very precious to me."

"When did you see it last?" asked the corporal, taking a notebook out of his pocket.

"Just before I left for the church supper. It was where it always is, in my jewel box on my bureau."

"What time was that?"

"Oh, I suppose it was a little after five-thirty. That's when the supper began and nearly everyone had already left for it."

Corporal Phelps jotted down something in his notebook. "Now tell me about when you came back, when you found it was gone."

"I was tired," said Aunt Emerald. "I left the fiesta after the raffles. Mr. Fisher, who boards across the road, came with me. I said good night to him and unlocked the door of the antique shop—my rooms are just above it—and I walked through the shop without turning on a light. When I got upstairs I went straight to my bureau and started to take off my necklace and I saw that my jewelry box was empty. I couldn't believe it. I went through all the drawers and even looked under the bed in a silly way, and then I hurried back to tell Adam."

"Was your jewelry insured?" inquired Corporal Phelps.

"Oh, yes," replied Aunt Emerald. "It was insured. But it isn't the value I'm thinking of. It couldn't be replaced in my heart for twenty times its value."

Cassie slid down on the edge of the couch and tucked her hand under Aunt Emerald's arm.

"Tell me, Mrs. Blomquist," continued the corporal, "is there anyone you can think of who might have done this? Anyone, maybe, who was jealous of all those jewels?"

"No one," declared Aunt Emerald positively. "No one at all."

"Very well. Now, who had the opportunity to break in after you left for the supper? Who came late or didn't come at all, can you remember?"

"The Rivers didn't either of them come," Cassie's father told him. "And both the men who board at the MacDougalls', Horace Bagley and Mr. Fisher, were late—in fact Mr. Fisher didn't come to the supper at all. But I've already searched their rooms—they asked me to—and there isn't anything there."

"They *asked* you to search their rooms?" said the corporal, making another note.

"Yes. I didn't think you'd object."

"Not at all, glad you did. Anyone else you can think of?"

"No, I don't believe so—except Gramma Banks next door, but she couldn't have done it."

"Why not?"

"Well, she's about ninety years old and sort of crazy, but perfectly innocent and good-hearted."

"Besides," said Cassie, "Fergus and I have already searched her house."

"You *what?*" demanded her father, and Corporal Phelps looked at her in surprise.

"Well, we thought maybe she took them because she likes bright-colored things. So we looked all over her house and they're not there."

"Of course not," declared Aunt Emerald.

The corporal stood up. "You won't mind if we just take another quick look, will you?" he said to Cassie. "Thank you, Mrs. Blomquist, that's all the questions for now. I'd like to see your room and the shop later on. I wonder if you'd write up a description of everything that's been taken, while I look around outside? Make it as detailed as you can."

He went to the door, accompanied by Cassie's father. "I'd like to talk to Bagley and Fisher first," he said as they went out. "Will you find them for me?"

Cassie exclaimed, "I didn't know he'd be a plainclothesman! He's nice, isn't he?"

"Very," Aunt Emerald agreed.

"I'm going out and hear what he says to Mr. Fisher and Mr. Bagley."

"He won't let you listen," said her mother. "Besides, you ought to be in bed."

"Oh, just let me *try*, Mom!"

Aunt Emerald said, "She'll never go to sleep with all the noise and excitement. Let her go."

"Well—but you mustn't bother the policemen, Cassie."

"I won't." Cassie gave Aunt Emerald a hug. "They'll find it, I know they will. You ought to see the trooper he's got with him. He's just great."

83

She dashed out the door.

The searchlight of the police car blazed on the front of The Rocking Horse. The yard was empty, the crowd dispersed, but little groups still stood at the edge of the shadows. Cassie could hear Corporal Phelps and Trooper Wallace talking from around the side of the shop where the window had been broken in. It was the window toward the back, shielded from the road by an old lilac bush. A sudden low hiss came from among the leaves of the maple tree. She looked up and saw Fergus' head hanging over the edge of the platform. He beckoned stealthily. Cassie sneaked to the tree and climbed up the ladder as quietly as she could. She was sure neither of the officers saw her.

"He made everyone go away," Fergus told her in a whisper. "He said they might be destroying evidence walking all over the grass. He told me to go to bed, but I outwitted him and got up here. Don't make a sound."

"I'm *not*," said Cassie under her breath.

They lay on their stomachs on the platform, trying to make themselves small and invisible.

Above them the dark branches of the tree loomed hugely up into the night; its leaves, lighted from below, were an artificial green. They could see everything the corporal and the gigantic trooper did at the window, hear every word of their conversation.

"I haven't found anything, Chief," Wallace said in his bass-drum voice. "The paint around this window's pretty worn and flaky. I doubt if it'll show up any fingerprints, and I'm afraid the grass is too dry for footprints."

Corporal Phelps was examining the windowsill. "What did you find out from Mrs. Rivers?" he asked.

"Well, she and her son had quite an argument. He wanted money from her—seems there's a payment due on his car, and the company's dunning him for it. He thought she had a lot hidden away, in a sock or somewhere. She told him she didn't and I gather she nagged at him to settle down and get a job around here, and he got mad and lit out. Did you get any information inside?"

"A little. Several people came late to the church

supper, including the old lady who lives next door and both the men who are boarding across the road. Mrs. Rivers didn't come at all."

"*She* could never have climbed in this window," said the trooper.

From across the road came Cassie's father and Mr. Bagley. Cassie and Fergus pulled in their heads and lay as still as stone while they walked almost under their tree and up to the officers.

"This is Mr. Bagley, Corporal," Cassie's father said. "Where do you want to talk to him?"

"Why don't we go around to the porch—we can sit down there. Willie, you go ahead and start the dusting, see if you can get any fingerprints, and then we'll want to rope off this area."

He led the way to the settle on the front porch and he and Cassie's father and Mr. Bagley sat down. Corporal Phelps took out his notebook. "Now, Mr. Bagley, where are you from?" he asked.

Mr. Bagley replied, "I'm from Wilton, Corporal, a suburb of Boston—143 Main Street. I've got a little apartment there, you can check with the superintendent, Mr. Kelly."

"And how did you happen to come here?"

"I was just driving around the countryside, looking for new localities to paint. I'd never been to Vermont before and I thought it was high time I saw it. Beautiful state! I just happened to drive into Dublin Center and I thought it was such a charming little village I'd just stay awhile."

Corporal Phelps wrote busily in his notebook.

"Now, about tonight," he said. "I understand you went late to the church supper."

"Yes, I was finishing up a painting—I wanted to get it done before the light changed."

"And after you finished it?"

"Well, now, let's see," said Mr. Bagley, rubbing his bald head. "I put away my paints and folded up my easel and then I went over to the MacDougalls' to leave them in my room." Mr. Bagley suddenly slapped his leg violently and sprang to his feet. Cassie and Fergus both jumped.

"How could I have forgotten it?" cried Mr. Bagley. "I saw it out of the window. A car stopped in front of Mrs. Blomquist's shop!"

"Go on," commanded Corporal Phelps.

"Well, I hardly paid any attention to it—I was busy putting my things away and washing up. I thought it was somebody stopping to look at antiques and that they'd drive on as soon as they found there wasn't anyone there."

"Was someone in the car when you saw it?"

"Yes, there were two people, a man and a woman. They must just have driven up when I noticed it, they hadn't even got out of the car yet. But it was gone when I came out."

Fergus whispered, "I bet *that's* who stole the jewelry, the people in the car!"

Cassie nodded, breathless with excitement.

Corporal Phelps went on with his questioning. "How long was it between the time you saw the car and the time you came out of the house?"

"Oh, quite a long time," replied Mr. Bagley. "I went down to the bathroom to wash my brushes—that takes a while—and then I changed my shirt because I'd got some paint on it. I suppose it was fifteen or twenty minutes anyway."

"And you didn't look out of the window again any of that time?"

"No, I didn't," said Mr. Bagley earnestly. "I was hurrying to get to the supper and not miss anything. I didn't even think of the car again after I saw it."

"Curious you didn't think about it before this," remarked the corporal, "after you heard the jewels had been stolen."

"It was stupid of me," said Mr. Bagley. "It just completely left my mind. You see at first I thought it must be that Rivers boy and then—well—"

"Never mind," interrupted Corporal Phelps. "What kind of car was it?"

"I'm afraid I'm not very knowledgeable about cars," said Mr. Bagley apologetically. "It might have been a Ford or a Chevy. It was dark gray, rather dirty, and I think it was a two-door sedan."

"Did you see the license plate?"

"No, I couldn't see it because the car was directly opposite my window and all I could see was the side."

"Don't you remember anything more about it? The tires, for instance, were they whitewall? How about an aerial?"

"The tires weren't whitewall, I'm sure of that,

but an aerial—now let me see." Mr. Bagley scratched his chin and thought. "Yes, there was one, I do remember now. It was on the right front fender, raised up quite high."

"Can you give me any description of the people?"

"Let me think, now," said Mr. Bagley. "The man was wearing a plaid shirt, I believe. I couldn't see the woman very well because she was on the far side—but I'm pretty sure she was wearing a little white hat."

"And that's all you remember?"

"Yes, it is," said Mr. Bagley regretfully. "I'm terribly sorry—if only I'd paid more attention!"

"Well, thank you very much," said Corporal Phelps. "Good night now."

Cassie and Fergus watched Mr. Bagley walk back across the road, shaking his head as he went.

Corporal Phelps said to Cassie's father, "Not much help on that description of the car. Let's talk to Fisher now. Will you get him?

"Well, at least we know there was a car," said Adam Clifford, getting up. "I didn't think it was anyone from around here, not even Red, really."

From the side of the house Trooper Wallace called, "Chief, come here, will you?"

The corporal joined him at the window. "What's up?" he asked.

"There are some very peculiar noises in that tree, sir," replied the trooper in his enormous voice. "I don't like the sound of them." He spun as quick as lightning to face the tree, his hand on his pistol.

"Don't shoot!" screamed Cassie. "It's just us!"

"Well, well," said Trooper Wallace, walking with measured steps to the tree. He flashed the beam of his torch straight at the platform. "Imagine finding you two up there. Why, I thought it was the jewel thief counting his loot."

Red-faced, they climbed down the ladder.

"Didn't you honestly know we were there all the time?" asked Fergus.

Trooper Wallace looked at them without a smile, but slowly, conspiratorially, he dropped the lid of one eye at them. Corporal Phelps laughed.

"Go to bed, you two," he said. "Come on, Wee Willie, we have work to do."

CHAPTER 7.

THE sun on her face awakened Cassie. She opened her eyes and saw that the clock on her table said nine o'clock. How *could* she have slept so late? Then she remembered last night—it had been midnight before she went to bed.

She had come into the house after their humiliating exposure in the tree and found her mother making coffee in the kitchen. "Those poor policemen," she said. "They'll need it. Why, they're going to be up half the night." Aunt Emerald was sitting at the table working over the list of jewelry.

"Oh, and there was the pearl brooch," she said to Cassie's mother. "Max bought the pearls from a little man in Tokyo, I remember him so well. He was about four feet tall and he called me Missy Bloom. We had them set in Rome in gold, in the shape of a star. And earrings to match. I loved those earrings."

"They'll find them, dear," Cassie's mother comforted her.

Cassie poured herself a glass of milk and ate a doughnut while sleepiness crept heavily over her. She fought against it, holding her eyes open in a wide unnatural stare, but her head would nod—and finally her mother took her to the foot of the stairs and gave her a friendly push. "Bed for you," she said, and, unable even to protest, Cassie had dragged herself up and fallen immediately fast asleep.

Now she leaped out of bed and tore downstairs barefooted. Her mother was ironing in the kitchen, and her father was standing at the front window drumming his fingers on the sill.

"What's happened?" cried Cassie. "Where's Aunt Emerald?"

"Stop fidgeting, Adam," said her mother. "They'll be here soon. Aunt Emerald's in the shop rearranging things—she's trying to keep busy, poor love. I think she wants to be alone. She didn't sleep a wink last night, and people have been coming around since breakfast bringing her cookies and pies and such, trying to show their sympathy."

"Just like a funeral," muttered her father.

"Well, it is sort of like one," said Cassie, "—all her beautiful jewelry that Uncle Max gave her. But what happened last night after I went to bed?"

"They interviewed Mr. Fisher first," her father told her, "and then Gramma Banks. She saw him come back from fishing, all right—it was pretty soon after Mr. Bagley left for the supper. But *he* says she was sitting on her front porch the whole time he was in the house, that he could see her from the kitchen while he was cleaning his fish, and *she* says she went in to feed her cats. So his alibi's not so watertight after all."

"But what about the car that stopped?" asked Cassie. "I thought they must have done it."

"Nobody actually saw them get out of the car.

Maybe they did just stop and then drive on again when they saw the shop was closed. Gramma Banks saw them drive by while she was out in the garden—saw the woman's white hat—but she couldn't see from around the side of her house what they did after they went by."

"Did they search Gramma Banks's house again?"

"Oh, sure—and Mr. Bagley's and Mr. Fisher's rooms and their cars, too. They didn't find a thing."

"I *still* think it was Red Rivers," said Cassie's mother. "He came roaring back last night, Cassie, right in the middle of their interviewing Gramma Banks—said he'd thought better of it and was ashamed of the way he treated his mother. Pretended he didn't know a thing about the robbery. I don't believe a word of it."

"But he wouldn't come back if he'd stolen it!" cried Cassie.

Her father said, "That's just what he would have done—after he'd disposed of it or hidden it somewhere." He struck his fist angrily on the windowsill. "Any one of them could have done it—Red Rivers or the people in the car or Mr. Bagley or Mr.

Fisher. Corporal Phelps seems to be quite interested in what *he* did after he came home from the fiesta with Aunt Emerald."

"What could he have done? It'd been stolen by then."

"I don't know," said her father, sounding irritable. "He says he went to his room and wrote a poem."

"Oh, dear!" said Cassie. "I thought of course it was the people in the car and that the police'd find them right away and everything would be all right."

"Well, they've sent out a general broadcast to all police agencies to watch for the car—the trouble is the description's so vague."

"I don't see how anyone could be so mean as to steal Aunt Emerald's jewelry!" Cassie burst out. "And how would they be able to sell it, anyway? The police have a description of what it all looks like."

"They'd turn it over to a fence—a person who receives stolen goods. He'd take all the jewels out of their settings and sell them individually." Her father's voice was morose.

"Oh, *no!*" cried Cassie. She thought of a horrible grimy man with mean little eyes, in a dark cellar, prying away, digging the emeralds and the sapphires, the diamonds, rubies, and pearls out of the necklaces and rings, smashing the gold that held them—destroying all the beautiful settings Uncle Max had designed. She felt like crying.

"What else happened last night?"

"They took a lot of pictures of the shop and Aunt Emerald's room, and they fingerprinted practically everybody and dusted for fingerprints."

"Oh, I *wish* I'd been here!" Cassie groaned. "Then they'd have fingerprinted me, too. Did they find any?"

"Just some glove prints on the bureau and jewelry box."

"*Glove* prints?"

"Sure, they can get them. They aren't too useful for identification—all they tell you is that the thief was wearing them and what material they were. These were leather."

Cassie went to the window beside her father and looked out. The road in front of the antique shop was roped off; there was just room for a car to get by on the far side of the stakes. "What have they done that for?" she asked.

"They're hoping to get some tire prints. That might help a little."

"Oh, I want to see them do that!" Cassie exclaimed.

"Well, if you want to see anything," said her mother, "you better go and get dressed quick. I'll have your breakfast ready when you come down."

Cassie flew through her dressing and her breakfast. She had just finished when the police car arrived. She dashed outdoors to find Fergus already there opening the door for the officers. Wallace grinned at them. "How are the tree-dwellers this morning?" he inquired. Cassie giggled, and Fergus blushed.

"Any report on the car?" her father asked Corporal Phelps.

"Not so far. I'm getting routine checks on Fisher and Bagley from New York and Boston. Now let's see if we're lucky enough to get any tire prints."

Trooper Wallace had already ducked under the ropes and was crouched at the side of the road. The corporal joined him.

"I didn't know they could take *tire* prints," said Cassie to Fergus. "How do they do it?"

"Plaster of Paris," Fergus told her. "They can do anything."

The two men examined the road carefully. Inch by inch they edged along. Occasionally Corporal Phelps took a lens out of his pocket and peered intently at the gravelly surface. Once he muttered, "Too darn many people scuffed around here last night."

They came to the end of the roped-off area. "Hoot!" rumbled Trooper Wallace and he stood up.

"What did you say?" said Fergus.

"I said 'Hoot.' It means I'm disgusted. No prints."

"But that's a Scottish word, isn't it?"

"Certainly it's Scottish. You ought to know, a boy with a good name like Fergus MacDougall."

"But are *you* Scottish?"

Corporal Phelps laughed. "He's convinced he's descended from William Wallace, national hero of Scotland—you know, 'Scots, wha hae wi' Wallace bled'? He's never been out of Vermont, but he's saving his pay to get to Scotland some day. Sometimes the old language just will break out."

"Now, Chief," said Trooper Wallace, looking hurt.

Corporal Phelps gave him an affectionate punch. "That's all right, Willie—I kind of like it. Now let's make that little experiment."

Together they removed the stakes and the ropes; then Corporal Phelps walked back to the police car while Wallace crossed the road and went into the MacDougalls' house. The corporal drove the car forward, parked it directly in front of the antique shop, slid over to the other side of the seat, lit his pipe, and sat there quietly smoking. Cassie and Fergus watched him with interest, wondering what was going to happen. Several minutes went by.

"What's the experiment going to be?" asked Cassie with a bounce of excitement.

Corporal Phelps winked at her. "We policemen

have to be mysterious, you know—no fun if we weren't."

Trooper Wallace came back out of the Mac-Dougalls' house and walked around to the side of the police car.

"How about it?" inquired the corporal.

The trooper shook his head. "No go," he said.

Cassie and Fergus looked at each other, mystified.

"Hm-m," said Corporal Phelps. He got out of the car. "I'm going to talk to Mrs. Banks again. You take another look around the window, Willie—maybe something will turn up that we missed last night." He and Cassie's father went off together to Gramma Banks's house.

Cassie and Fergus followed Trooper Wallace around the side of the antique shop. There were more ropes here, enclosing the lilac bush and a large area around the window.

"Can we help you hunt?" begged Cassie.

"Sure," said Wallace. "You've got bright young eyes, you just might come on something. We're going over every blade of this grass."

All three of them dropped to their hands and knees. The trooper looked like a gigantic bear, but he moved his hands over the grass as searchingly and methodically as a surgeon. Cassie and Fergus tried to imitate him. Oh, thought Cassie, if only I'd find something—a button, maybe, or a bobby pin that had fallen out of the woman's hair, the woman with the white hat. *Anything* would be a help—the police could trace the thieves from the tiniest little thing. Particularly Corporal Phelps and Trooper Wallace.

"Uh-h," said Fergus. "I've got a grandmother in Scotland." He's just showing off, thought Cassie, trying to make the trooper like him.

"Good," said Trooper Wallace. "You keep in touch with her. The MacDougalls are a fine old clan. Do you know what your crest is?"

"Crest?" said Fergus, sounding baffled.

"Certainly—all the clans have crests. Some of them even have war cries. I'll look it up for you in a book I have at home."

"War cries—gee!" said Fergus. "My gram sends me things sometimes."

"She sent him a kilt," said Cassie. "He thought it was a skirt."

The trooper looked shocked.

"I didn't really," said Fergus quickly. "I was just pretending."

"You should wear your kilt proudly," declared Wallace. "It's a beautiful costume. I wear mine when I'm not in uniform."

Cassie tried to imagine Trooper Wallace, that enormous man, in a kilt. It was beyond her imagination—she could only think of him, magnificent, in his police uniform. Fergus gulped, and Cassie could see him mentally adjusting his opinion of kilts.

"You wear your kilt," the trooper went on, while his huge hands continued to slide over the grass, "and some day I'll come out and play the bagpipes for you and teach you to do the sword dance."

This was really too much for Fergus. "You don't *dance,* do you?" he pleaded.

Trooper Wallace gave Fergus a reproving glance. With dignity he rose to his full majestic height. He towered above Cassie and Fergus sitting on their heels. Without a word he ducked under the

ropes and laid two sticks crosswise on the ground;
then he placed one hand on his belt and arched the
other over his head. Nimbly, gracefully, with aston-
ishing speed, his booted feet flashed over and between the sticks, never touching them. As suddenly
as he had begun he stopped, kicked the sticks away,
and returned to his search.

"Beautiful," said a voice from the window. "I haven't seen it done since I was in Scotland years ago. It used to make me cry, it was so exciting."

There was Aunt Emerald looking out at them. She was smiling, and Cassie felt a surge of gratitude to Trooper Wallace for making her think of something beside her heartache.

"Thank you, ma'am," he beamed. "It's better with a sword and scabbard, of course."

Corporal Phelps and Cassie's father came across the grass to them.

"Well, Wee Willie," said the corporal. "I saw you doing your little dance. Is that the way you act when you're supposed to be investigating a felony?"

"Sorry, sir," apologized Wallace, slightly red. "I got a little carried away because the boy was taking a dim view of the Scottish dances." He became all state trooper, very official. "There's nothing here, sir. I've been over every inch of the grass."

"Too bad," said the corporal. "I didn't get far with Mrs. Banks either. She can't remember now whether it was yesterday or the day before that she saw the car, but she still says she went in to feed her cats while Mr. Fisher was in the MacDougalls' house. And she thinks I'm such a nice young man that she's going to name her pig 'Phelps' after me." He grimaced and lit his pipe.

"I think it's a great honor," said Wallace seriously. He turned his head and winked slyly at Cassie and Fergus. Aunt Emerald laughed from the window.

Cassie switched idly with a stick at the long grass under the lilac. A glimmer of something half hidden under a dead leaf caught her eye. She reached in her hand and brushed the leaf away.

"Oh, Aunt *Emerald!*" she shouted—and she picked up a pearl earring set in gold like a little star.

Corporal Phelps pounced. "Don't handle it," he commanded. He flicked a handkerchief out of his pocket and dropped it over the earring in Cassie's hand. Carefully he lifted it up and turned it over onto his palm, still lying on the handkerchief. He stepped toward the window with his hand outstretched.

"Yours, Mrs. Blomquist?"

Aunt Emerald nodded. She stared at the earring,

with her face twisted as though she were going to cry.

"Whoever went through the window with your jewelry dropped it," said Corporal Phelps, "and it rolled under the bush. I'm sorry, Mrs. Blomquist, I'll have to take it in for fingerprints, but I'll get it back to you as soon as I can."

Aunt Emerald nodded again. Her face broke into a tremulous smile.

"Thank you for finding it, Cassie darling," she said.

CHAPTER 8.

SO Cassie got fingerprinted after all. Corporal Phelps did it before he and Wallace drove away. He rolled her fingers on an inky slab and then pressed them down onto a piece of paper: there, as clear as could be, was the imprint of the fine swirly lines from each of her fingers.

"Now we won't mix your prints up with the thief's," he told her.

"And remember," said Trooper Wallace darkly, "we've got your prints on file, so you better not go committing any crimes."

Cassie could see that Fergus was jealous of her for getting fingerprinted—he watched the process intently, but she knew he didn't quite dare ask them to do it to him. Well, she thought smugly, it just makes up for his thinking he's so special with his Scottish grandmother.

They climbed up in the tree after the police car drove away—it was the best place to talk over all the excitement. Cassie told him everything her father had told her about the night before. Fergus produced a pad of paper and a pencil.

"We ought to write down the list of suspects," he said. "And the times and everything—that's very important."

"Okay," said Cassie. "Put down the people in the car first."

"What time did Mr. Bagley see them?"

"He said it was about twenty minutes before he came to the supper. That was about quarter past six, I guess. Put down five fifty-five."

Fergus wrote, "5:55 PM: dirty gray car, Ford or Chevy with aerial, stops in front of Rocking Horse, with man wearing plaid shirt, woman wearing white hat. Seen by Mr. Bagley (and Gramma Banks?)."

"Now put down Mr. Bagley," said Cassie.

"No, we ought to have Red Rivers in first. He's *much* more likely. I wish we knew what time it was we saw him drive by. I know it was after Mr. Fisher came."

"Just put 'after supper,'" suggested Cassie.

Fergus wrote, "After supper (time indefinite): Red Rivers leaves town in hurry—looks funny."

"Now put Mr. Bagley," said Cassie. "He was painting when we left—that was just after five-thirty."

"Call it five-forty," said Fergus and he added to his list, "5:40: Mr. Bagley is painting in front of Rocking Horse. 6:15: he arrives church supper."

Cassie looked at what he had written. "That gave him plenty of time."

"It gave him time to steal it," said Fergus, "but it didn't give him time to bury it. And he'd *have* to of, or they'd have found it in his room or car. Now we've just got Mr. Fisher left."

"It's kind of confusing about him," said Cassie. "If he's telling the truth about Gramma Banks being on her front porch all the time, he wouldn't have *dared* go over. But she says she went in to feed her cats."

"Suppose he's lying," said Fergus. "Suppose he saw her go back in the house and just dashed across the road and broke in. He could steal the jewelry and be back in just a few minutes, while she was still inside."

"Write down the times, anyway," said Cassie. "He got back from fishing just after Mr. Bagley left. Say it was twenty minutes past six."

Fergus wrote, "6:20: Mr. Fisher returns from fishing. Seen by Gramma Banks."

"Now put down what time he got to the fiesta. He said it was seven o'clock and that was just about the time we met him at the soft-drink place, so that's okay."

Fergus looked thoughtfully at what he had written. "Gee," he said, "that doesn't give him any more time than it does Mr. Bagley. Forty minutes isn't enough time to steal it and bury it, too."

Cassie had a sudden flash of inspiration.

"Listen, Fergus!" she cried, wide-eyed. *"That's*

why he left the fiesta early with Aunt Emerald. He'd stolen it before he came and just left it in his room, and he had all that time to hide it before she discovered it and got it reported! Dad *said* Corporal Phelps was specially interested in what he did after he came home."

Fergus stared at her. "How about that?" he said, and whistled quietly.

"And all this time he's been fishing," Cassie rushed on, "he could have found *hundreds* of good places to hide it along the stream back of your house. He could just have gone out your back door and crept down there and still gotten back in plenty of time."

"That's brilliant, Cassie," said Fergus admiringly.

Cassie blushed with pride.

They could see Henry, the goat, and Phelps, the pig, in Gramma Banks's back yard. Henry was walking in a circle around Phelps, who revolved slowly to keep facing him. The goat's head was lowered, his horns pointing at the pig's tempting fatness, but quite suddenly Phelps let out such a loud and terrifying snort that Henry jumped straight into the air and several feet backward.

Both children laughed aloud.

"Good for Phelps!" Fergus said.

The door opened and Gramma Banks stepped out with her crow perched on her shoulder. She was carrying a basket, and Cassie could count four layers of aprons that hung one below another over her dress. The goat walked away from her and stood moodily in the corner with his leathery lower lip stuck out.

"Now, dearie," she addressed the pig, "Gramma's going off for a little. Don't be lonely—Henry will take care of you."

"He'll take care of Henry, you mean," Fergus chuckled.

Gramma Banks went through the gate and across the field in back of her house that stretched up to the woods. Three cats came after her; they jumped at grasshoppers, they leaped high in the air to bat at butterflies, they did everything to pretend they were not following her and that it was entirely their own idea to take a small walk in the fields at that exact moment. The crow took off from her shoulder and flew, cawing, ahead of her. Cassie and Fergus watched Gramma Banks. Occasionally she took a few little running steps, almost a dance; at other times she glanced swiftly over her shoulder. There was something partly triumphant, partly furtive about her progress.

"Where on earth's she going?" said Fergus.

"And what's she going to do?" added Cassie.

Gramma Banks came to the little brook that ran through the field. Her aprons flapped as she jumped over it: she looked like a scrawny ungainly bird learning to fly. She turned and peered behind her. Then, skipping and hopping, she made her way toward the woods. One after another the cats leaped the brook and continued their disinterested stroll.

Cassie and Fergus were puzzled.

"There isn't anything up in the woods except the sugar house," Fergus said. "What's she want to go there for?"

"And what's she got that basket for?" Cassie asked. "There aren't any wildflowers or nuts in the woods this time of year."

"Mushrooms, maybe?" Fergus suggested.

"She's scared of mushrooms, she told me so once. She said they could be deadly poison."

They stared after the small diminishing figure of Gramma Banks. She must be planning to put something in the basket, thought Cassie, something pretty, something bright. Something——

"*Fergus!*" gasped Cassie. "Do you suppose she did steal Aunt Emerald's jewelry after all and she's got it hidden up there in the sugar house?"

Fergus let out a low whistle. "And she's going to bring it down in the basket now, you mean?"

Cassie nodded soberly. "She *was* the last person to come to the fiesta, you know."

It was an appalling thought that Gramma Banks, so kindhearted she wouldn't hurt a fly, had stolen the jewelry and actually hidden it. They looked at each other in dismay.

"Probably she was scared they'd take it away from her if she kept it in the house," said Cassie after a minute. "But that makes it so much worse that she's hidden it! What'll they do to her, put her in jail?"

"I guess." Fergus nodded. "We ought to tell your father." He sounded reluctant.

"Maybe we could persuade her to put it back," Cassie said. "Then they wouldn't put her in jail."

"Maybe we could," agreed Fergus. "Let's follow her up there."

They climbed down from the tree and started across the field. Gramma Banks had disappeared over a little rise of land. Beyond was the woods and at the edge of the woods was the sugar house where, every spring, Cassie's father boiled the maple sap till it turned from thin colorless liquid into golden syrup. Cassie and Fergus came to the top of the hill. There was no sign of Gramma Banks; all they could see was the little gray house tucked cozily beside the woods. Unconsciously they slowed and began to tiptoe as they drew near.

They could hear a remote sound of hammering and the barking of a dog from the village behind them, but the field and the woods were silent in a summer drowse. From the branch of a dead pine tree the crow stared down at them, unblinking, with his black eyes. Suddenly he ruffled his feathers, hunched his shoulders, and let out a harsh abusive squawk.

Cassie jumped. "Sh-sh!" she quavered.

Silently they crept to the window. It was dusty and cobwebby, and the sun on the panes made it impossible for them to see anything but their own reflections. They cupped their hands beside their faces and pressed close to the glass. Gradually they began to see the inside of the dark room—the big firebox, the trays for boiling. In a corner knelt Gramma Banks with her basket beside her.

But instead of seeing what they expected to see— her hands gloating over Aunt Emerald's jewelry— they saw that she held a baby's nursing bottle and that what she was bent over, lying in a nest of burlap bags lined with grass, was a little fawn, tawny and dappled.

"*Oh!*" said Cassie out loud, in a mixture of disappointment and relief.

Gramma Banks looked quickly up at the window. Her wrinkled old face broke into a smile and she beckoned to them. They ran in the door to where she knelt. The fawn looked at them with enormous eyes and sucked on.

"I thought you was your pa, Cassie," Gramma Banks said, "come to take Gramma's new baby away from her."

"Oh, he wouldn't do that, Mrs. Banks," objected Cassie.

"He might, bein' game warden and all."

"Where's its mother?" asked Fergus.

"Shot by poachers, I wouldn't doubt. I found it all alone in the woods yesterday. Waited and watched I did, real secret, but she never come back. So I just picked it up in my arms, it don't weigh hardly nothin', and I carried it here where it'd be safe and I could take care of it."

"Oh, it's so *darling!*" Cassie exclaimed. "Why don't you take it down to the house?"

Gramma Banks stroked the top of the fawn's autumn-leaf head. "It's better here," she said. "It can smell the woods and hear owls at night. Feels more at home, like."

Cassie looked down at the old woman and the small fawn. She felt tender toward them both. "Could I feed it, do you think?" she asked.

Gramma Banks nodded, and Cassie knelt beside

her and took the bottle from her. "Hold it upright, now, so it don't swallow no air," said Gramma.

The fawn pulled steadily on the nipple, moving its big ears back and forth as it sucked, and the milk sank lower and lower in the bottle.

"Hungry, ain't you, dear heart?" said Gramma. "Now I'm goin' to get some leaves and grass to freshen up your bed."

"I'll get it," said Fergus. He grabbed the basket and ran out the door. In a minute he was back with a basketful of grass and ferns and leaves stripped from the maples. The fawn got jerkily to its feet and stood swaying slightly while they lined the warm hollow in the burlap bags with the sweet-smelling greenery.

"You'll be eatin' this soon," said Gramma Banks. "Nibblin' away in the woods just like a big deer. But while you're so new, Gramma'll take care of you."

"Can I help you, Mrs. Banks?" begged Cassie. "Can I come up here every day with you and help take care of it?"

"You could," said Gramma Banks.

"Uh—could I, too?" asked Fergus.

Gramma Banks looked at him narrowly. "Boys is too rough," she said.

"He got the grass and stuff," Cassie reminded her.

"So he did now." Gramma's eyes turned kind. "And he was real gentle, too. Yes, he can come. But don't you tell the other kids, now—I don't want them traipsin' up here, botherin' and gawkin'."

"We won't," Cassie and Fergus promised.

The fawn lay down again on the soft bed. It curled itself into a ball, gave them one melting look, and went to sleep.

"Oh," whispered Cassie, "I love it so!"

They all stood up and tiptoed out the door. One by one from the woods the three cats appeared and rubbed themselves in a purring circle against Gramma Banks's legs. The crow flapped down from the pine tree to light on her shoulder.

The sun was bright after the dusk of the sugar house—it made the white houses of the village below them gleam. Cassie saw her mother hanging sheets on the line in the back yard, she saw the neat rows of their vegetable garden, and Patience, the cow, steadily grazing in the pasture. Everything looked the way it always looked, but Cassie suddenly remembered how different it was. Aunt Emerald was in the antique shop, rearranging things, because she wanted to be alone. It was silly of her and Fergus to have thought Gramma Banks had stolen the jewelry—it was probably hidden somewhere along the brook under the low-hanging alder bushes or among the rocks, where no one could find it.

As though voicing Cassie's thought, Gramma Banks said, "I just hate to think of all your Aunt Emerald's pretty things gone." Her eyes filled with tears. "Did me good every time I looked at her all bright and glittery. I'd give her a string of my beads to cheer her up, but 'twouldn't be the same. You think those policemen will find out who did it?"

"Sure they will," said Fergus.

"It was Mr. Fisher, *we* think," Cassie said.

"No-o," said Gramma Banks slowly. "It comes to my mind now I fed my cats *after* he went down to the church. I'm pretty sure I was a-settin' on the porch the whole time."

Cassie and Fergus gaped at her.

"Then it *must* have been the people in the car or Red Rivers," said Fergus.

"Musta been," said Gramma Banks. "You comin' home now?"

But Cassie didn't want to go back just yet; she wanted to do something that would take her mind off Aunt Emerald's misery. "Let's go up to the deserted castle," she said to Fergus. "We haven't been there for a long time."

"Okay," Fergus agreed. "We can get to it the back way through the woods."

"Good-bye, then, children," said Gramma Banks. "Bring me a pink stone if you find one in the brook." She fluttered her hand at them as a child does and started down the hill. The crow rode proudly on her shoulder, and behind her, Indian file, went the cats.

CHAPTER 9.

THE deserted castle was not really a castle, but it was so tall and angular, so ornamented with gables and porches and balconies, that Cassie and Fergus liked to pretend that it was.

It had been built by an eccentric German named Zimmerman who loved deep woods and elaborate architecture; he had even added a turret with an onion-shaped dome to remind him of his native Bavaria. Scattered about the clearing and peering out from the trees at its edge were carved stone figures of little gnomelike men with long beards. Mr. Zimmerman had used the house as a hunting lodge, entertaining large groups of hearty sportsmen in its ample rooms.

But that was long ago: it had been empty for years and its windows were boarded up. Cassie's father, the only real-estate agent in Dublin Center, occasionally tried to sell it to someone looking for a summer camp, but it was so remote and so falling into disrepair that no one was interested in it for long. An old bumpy road led steeply up to it, getting closer and closer to the mountain behind it, and died away at its doorstep after having crossed a bridge over a roaring stream.

The house had seemed a secret and half-scary place to Cassie and Fergus when they first found they could get into it, but by now they were quite accustomed to it and, consequently, brave. Only occasionally did Cassie's heart thump wildly when, in a dark room, a shutter banged or a dead leaf rustled, ghostlike, in a corner.

They scrambled through the woods back of the sugar house, climbing up at an angle to reach the old lodge. The earth was spongy with rotted leaves and moss, patterned with creeping ground pine.

"Gramma Banks is nice," remarked Cassie. "I'm not going to call her Batty Hattie any more."

"But she really is, sort of," said Fergus.

"I know. But 'batty' sounds kind of looking down your nose. Just 'cause she's *different*—"

"You could call her Catty Hattie because of all her cats."

"No, 'catty' isn't nice either."

"How about Hammy Grammy? Except that pig won't ever be ham."

"Oh, Fergus!" Cassie laughed. She thought awhile. "From now on I'm going to call you Frugal MacDougall."

"What does frugal mean?"

"Sort of stingy, I think."

"I'm *not* stingy. If you call me that I'll call you Grassy Cassie or Stiff-Board Clif-ford."

"Well, then, Bugle MacDougall," said Cassie. "Do you like that better?"

"Sure, except I haven't got a bugle. I'm going to learn to play the bagpipes."

"I suppose you think Trooper Wallace will teach you?"

"Of course he'll teach me."

"Well, I don't want to be anywhere around when you start screeching on those things."

"It's a beautiful instrument," said Fergus with dignity.

"You've gotten awfully Scottish in the last day, it seems to me," Cassie said.

"I didn't know how great they were," said Fergus reverently.

They were panting from the climb when the woods thinned to a clearing and there, gaunt and weathered and lofty, was the deserted castle. The brook raged down the hill past it; its spray bounced on the bridge and sparkled on the crumbling wood.

"No one better drive a car over that bridge," observed Fergus. "It's going down pretty soon."

They crossed it one at a time. Cassie held her muscles rigid and tried to make herself as light as possible as she tiptoed across.

"Do you think we can still get in that window?" she asked.

"Sure," Fergus said. "There wouldn't have been anybody up here to fix it."

They walked through the overgrown grass to the front steps where a little stone man grinned at them. Cassie patted the top of his peaked hat. "We won't hurt anything," she told him softly.

The porch ran all around the house, actually overhanging the brook on one side, and here there was a window with a loose shutter and a broken pane. Carefully Fergus reached his hand through the opening and turned the rusty lock; the window groaned stiffly as he pushed it up. He clambered through, and Cassie followed him.

They stood in the old living room, empty and dusky, smelling faintly of pine boards and kerosene. At one end of the room was a huge stone fireplace, and over it hung the bearded, glowering head of an enormous moose. One of its yellow glass eyes was missing and its fur was patchy.

"I wouldn't want to meet him on a dark night," remarked Fergus.

"Poor old thing," Cassie said. "He looks worse every time we come. Where did Mr. Zimmerman get him, anyway? There aren't any moose around here."

"I bet he bought it," Fergus said.

"Maybe they were roaming the land in the olden days when he lived here."

"Nuts," said Fergus. "He bought it from a junk dealer."

They stared at the somber face, and the moose stared back at them with his one eye. Suddenly a weird, harsh chattering came from the chimney. Cassie jumped and grabbed Fergus. For a horrible moment she thought the moose had come to life and that it was his threatening voice they heard. Then from the fireplace opening the bright-eyed face of a red squirrel peeked down and around at them.

Cassie took a deep, relieved breath.

"Oh, you scared me, squirrel!" she gasped.

Fergus laughed. "Is he ever mad! He thinks he owns this place."

The face disappeared—there was the flick of an angry tail and a scrabbling noise ascending the chimney.

"Let's see if there are any more baby mice in that

bureau," suggested Cassie. She led the way to the rickety staircase in the front hall.

Upstairs in one of the gloomy, shuttered bedrooms there was an old chest of drawers. Cassie pulled open the bottom one as quietly as she could, and there in the corner was a soft pile of dried milkweed fluff and grasses and something that had certainly once been moose fur. Curled on it were four hairless little pink shapes.

"Oh, there *are!*" exclaimed Cassie. "They must be just brand-new, they're so pink."

"They're pretty disgusting," observed Fergus.

"I love them. They're so tiny and they curl up so cutely with their tails around them."

"Go ahead and touch one," said Fergus. "I bet you don't dare."

"I do so," said Cassie. She reached out her hand and touched one of the small bodies with one finger. The mouse stirred slightly, and Cassie drew her hand back quickly.

"It's so *bare*-feeling," she said.

Fergus howled with laughter.

"You be quiet," said Cassie. "They'll be *dar-*

ling when they get their fur. Just wait and see."

They watched the bare pink mice for a minute and then Fergus said, "Let's go up in the onion tower."

"Okay," agreed Cassie, and she shut the drawer.

The entrance to the tower was through a door in the corner of the living room, and, inside, a staircase went spiraling upward. It was dark and eerie in spite of the slit of a window halfway up. Cassie's heart always beat a little faster as she climbed the creaking stairs, but it was worth it when you got to the top. A trapdoor opened onto a round platform. There was another window here, and from it you could see the tops of the trees, the course of the rocky tumbling brook, the toy village in the gentle valley below. The ceiling of the tower flared out and then narrowed to a point above their heads: it had once been painted bright blue and speckled with golden stars. It was faded now, but still gay. Cassie felt delightfully small and floating up here, as though she were inside a Christmas ornament. She knew Fergus would be scornful of this idea if she mentioned it, so instead she said, "Let's pretend we've just discovered helium and invented the balloon and we're sailing away on a trial flight."

Fergus was staring intently out the window. "Listen," he said. "Doesn't that sound like a car?"

They both saw it at the same moment, an old car coming slowly up the bumpy road. It stopped at the far side of the bridge.

"How funny!" exclaimed Cassie. "Who in the world would be coming up here?"

A man they had never seen got out and walked forward to examine the bridge and then beckoned to someone else in the car. The door opened, and a woman stepped out. She was wearing a print dress and a white hat—and suddenly Cassie caught her breath in horror.

"Fergus!" she gasped. "It's *them!* It's the man and the woman and the car!"

"Yeeps!" said Fergus.

"That *is* the car—see, it's a Ford and it's got an aerial and it's dark gray and dirty—and the woman's wearing a white hat!"

"But the man's got a blue shirt on—Mr. Bagley said it was plaid."

"He's just *changed* it!" cried Cassie in an agony of excitement and terror. "They hid the jewels here yesterday and now they've come to get them!"

The man and the woman walked cautiously across the bridge. Cassie's heart hammered inside her and her throat felt dry.

"It's them, all right," said Fergus. His face was quite pale. "If only we knew where they'd hidden it, maybe we could get it before they got in, and then hide ourselves."

"But we *don't*," moaned Cassie. "It would take us too long to find it, and they'd find *us*. Oh, what'll we *do*?"

Fergus suddenly, frantically, began to pry up the trapdoor. "We've got to get word to your Dad," he said wildly. "We've got to get out of here before they get in and not let them see us, and then we'll run as fast as we can. Come on!"

He was already dashing down the curving stairs. Cassie came after him in a panic. Her thoughts raced and tumbled like her heart—what if they couldn't get out in time?—what if the people found them?—what would they *do* to them?

They flung themselves through the door at the bottom of the stairs and across the room to the open window.

"Go on through!" said Fergus in a low, tight voice. He grabbed her shoulder and pushed her at the window. Cassie had one leg over the sill and was just ducking her head to go through when a noise came from the hall, the unmistakable noise of a key turning in a squeaky lock. Terrified, Cassie raised her head on the outside of the window and looked straight into the face of the woman in the white hat, coming toward her along the porch.

Cassie hurled herself back through the window, knocking Fergus down and falling on top of him. She was so stiff with fright that she couldn't move, and there they lay in a heap on the floor while the front door opened, letting in a flood of light, and into the room walked the unknown man.

He stopped abruptly when he saw them, and at the same moment the head of the woman appeared outside the window, peering in.

"What's happening?" she said.

Cassie disentangled herself from Fergus. She

was shaking all over, and her hands felt clammy.

"What are you kids doing here?" said the man.

Fergus stood up. He faced the man and said bravely, even though his voice was high, "We know what you're here for."

"What?" said the man.

"The jewels you stole. We know you did it."

Cassie was somewhat emboldened by Fergus' courage; she clutched his ankle for reassurance and quavered defiantly, "And whatever you do to us, they'll catch you."

The man scratched his head and screwed up his face. He spoke to the woman at the window. "My dear Emmy, it seems we are jewel thieves."

"What *are* they talking about?" said the woman.

They're just pretending, thought Cassie, trying to stall us off. Oh, if only one of us could get away and run for help! But she couldn't see how to do it while the man stood between them and the doorway, and the woman blocked the window. Maybe if they both ran at the man together. . . . She got shakily to her feet.

"Fergus—" she whispered.

But before she could even try to get her plan across to him the sound of another car came from outside. A door slammed and they heard footsteps on the bridge. Cassie felt her stomach turn over in a mixture of hope and fear.

The man struck his hand to his forehead. "We are lost!" he said. "The deputy sheriff is here. Shall I help you through that window, Emmy, or do you want to come around by the porch and give yourself up?"

Cassie didn't even stop to think how funny this sounded; she heard the words "deputy sheriff" and her heart leaped high. She flew across the room as her father came in the door.

"Dad!" she shouted. "It's the man and the woman! They've hidden it here!"

Her father looked surprised but unconcerned. "Why, Cassie, what are you doing here?" he said.

Cassie grabbed his arm. *"Arrest* them, Dad! They're the jewel thieves!"

"You're crazy, Cassie," said her father calmly. "This is Mr. and Mrs. Peterson from New Jersey."

"I don't *care* what their name is or where they're

from!" cried Cassie. "Can't you *see* how they answer the description? She's got a white hat on and the car's the exact one Mr. Bagley saw!"

Fergus had quietly crossed the room. Now he stood beside Cassie's father, glaring at the man, with his hands in fists. "I'll help you if they make any trouble, Mr. Clifford."

"Now you two just calm down," said Cassie's father, "and stop insulting Mr. and Mrs. Peterson. They're looking for a summer place—the bank in town sent them to me—and I thought they might be interested in the lodge. I sent them on ahead because Patience had broken the fence and I had to finish mending it before she got out."

"But the *description!*" Cassie persisted.

"Use your head, Cassie," said her father. "There're a hundred cars that fit that description, and everyone wears a white hat in summer. And why on earth would they come to *me* if they had anything to do with it?"

Cassie thought this over. It was certainly convincing. She looked at Mr. Peterson and at Mrs. Peterson, who had just come in the door. His face was merry and kind, and hers was motherly. Cassie began to feel deflated.

"But why did he say, 'We are lost?'" she demanded, unable to give up a last shred of suspicion.

"He's just a ham actor," said Mrs. Peterson, smiling at her. "He can't resist a bit of play-acting."

"I thought it was very convincing," said Mr. Peterson. "But has there really been a robbery?"

"Yes," Cassie's father answered. "Somebody stole all my wife's aunt's jewelry last night, and a car was seen with a man and a woman in it."

"Oh, how dreadful!" exclaimed Mrs. Peterson.

"And you really thought we were the thieves?" Mr. Peterson asked Cassie and Fergus. They both nodded.

"Then I think you're extremely brave children standing up to us the way you did. I'd be proud of you if you were mine." He shook hands with them both.

"Mercy, yes," said Mrs. Peterson. "I'd have been scared to death."

"I was," said Cassie.

"Me, too," admitted Fergus.

140

Cassie added disconsolately, "Oh, dear, this is the third time we've thought we were going to find Aunt Emerald's jewelry for her."

Her father said, "Just stop being detectives and leave that up to Corporal Phelps." He turned to the Petersons. "Do you want to look around now, since I'm not going to arrest you after all?"

"Yes," said Mrs. Peterson eagerly. "It's the most beautiful location I've ever seen. Don't you think so, Julian?"

"It's quite a spot. And I bet there's good fishing in that brook where it's quieter, isn't there?" Mr. Peterson said to Cassie's father.

"Oh, yes, the fishing's fine. I'll show you around the house now."

"You won't hurt the baby mice in the bureau drawer, will you?" begged Cassie.

"Don't worry," said Mrs. Peterson. And she added firmly, "We won't even open it."

CHAPTER 10.

CASSIE and Fergus said good-bye to the Petersons and left them with Cassie's father. They crossed the bridge and walked down the road.

"Gee," said Fergus, "I really thought we'd found where the jewels were this time."

Cassie sighed. "I did, too. It was awful scary for a while, wasn't it?"

"Uh-*huh!*" agreed Fergus. "I wonder if the Petersons'll buy that place."

"I hope they do. Then they'd fix it up and it'd be nice again, not all falling to pieces and lonely."

"We couldn't go there any more, though."

"Of course we could," said Cassie. "We'd go call on them and I bet they'd give us root beer and cookies. That's the kind of people I think they are."

As they came into the village they saw that men were taking down the strings of lights and the streamers at the church green. Red Rivers, pale and subdued, waved at them; Cassie thought his hair didn't even look as red as usual.

Fergus dropped off to help, and Cassie walked on, anxious to see how Aunt Emerald was feeling now. She stopped on the porch of The Rocking Horse to pat Mr. Gallup's head. "Don't worry," she said, "Aunt Emerald won't sell you." Idly she wondered what old treasure of hers was still inside him and had started to take off his saddle to investigate when Aunt Emerald's voice called, "Come up and see me, Cassie dear."

Cassie ran through the shop and up the stairs. Aunt Emerald was sitting in a rocking chair by the window and at first Cassie didn't know what was so strange about her appearance. Then she realized that it was because she was not wearing any jewelry

—ever since Cassie could remember her she had been bedecked with bright stones, glowing with color.

"Oh-h," said Cassie mournfully.

"I'm sitting here trying to be philosophical," said Aunt Emerald, "and trying to get used to myself without my finery."

"But you've still got your rubies," said Cassie. "They weren't stolen."

"But they're all I have got. I think I better save them in case they never find the rest."

"Oh, they'll find them, Aunt Emerald! They've just *got* to!"

Aunt Emerald smiled at her. "Keep hoping, Cassie dear."

"We thought we'd found them for you—*twice* we thought so," said Cassie. She sat down on the floor and told about following Gramma Banks to the sugar house and about the little fawn. "Oh, it was *so* cute," she said. "But I wish it could have been your jewelry instead." She went on with the account of the deserted lodge and their excitement and terror when they saw the car and the people.

"But," she finished, "they turned out to be just Mr. and Mrs. Peterson from New Jersey and they're awfully nice after all. Oh, Aunt Emerald, maybe they'll buy the house and want to furnish it all in antiques and they'll buy them all from *you!*"

"That would be delightful," said Aunt Emerald. "Is that their car driving by now?"

Cassie got up on her knees and looked out the window. "Yes, it is. That means Dad'll be home in a minute. I'm going down and wait for him and see if they bought it. As soon as I find out I'll come back and tell you."

"Do," said Aunt Emerald. "I like your company."

Cassie trotted down the stairs into the antique shop. She remembered that she hadn't dusted it for several days and ran her finger experimentally over the top of a spinet: it left a definite groove on the surface. I'll just do a little dusting, thought Cassie, while I wait for Dad. She got the feather duster out of a cupboard and began to flick it over the furniture, thinking sadly about Aunt Emerald and her beautiful, stolen jewelry. I hope those awful people haven't broken it all up yet—oh, let the police catch them before that! . . . A little disloyal voice inside her said, "Maybe it was Red Rivers after all." Could it have been? She shook the thought away from her. She and Fergus had been so sure it was Mr. Fisher, but Gramma Banks had been sitting on her front porch all the time. . . . Or *had* she? Was she mixed up again?

The thought of Mr. Fisher reminded Cassie of the clock he wanted to buy. She glanced up at it standing on its shelf where she had seen it and loved it for so long. The round face looked down at her and beneath it the little figures of Hansel and Gretel ran through the woods. That old witch will never catch them, thought Cassie—and yet, oddly, it seemed to her as if the witch had emerged farther from her doorway in pursuit of the children. And could it be?—yes, it was!—Hansel and Gretel had moved on, too. She used to be able to see their faces and now all she could see was the backs of their heads and their flying heels.

"It's *going* again!" exclaimed Cassie in delight. But she looked once more at the clock face and saw that the hands still stood at exactly four minutes past eleven, just as they always had.

"How *funny!*" she said, as she pulled a chair against the wall and climbed on it. She turned her ear toward the clock and listened intently. There was no ticking, no whirring, no sound whatsoever from it; and there was no vibration in the little figures. They were still as stone in their new positions, moved on as though by magic.

"But how *could* they?" said Cassie.

She stood on tiptoe on the chair and tried to peer into the opening behind the figures. But she couldn't see inside, it was too dark. They revolved on a little wooden platform and below it was a deep space hidden by the front of the case, which, Cassie knew, held the mechanism to make them run. She thought, I bet a mouse got in there and built a nest and that's what moved them. She reached her hand carefully around the witch into the opening and stretched it downward over the edge of the platform. Immediately the tips of her fingers felt something soft. She poked at it and realized that it was absorbent cotton.

"That would make a good nest," thought Cassie.

"I wonder where they found it? Are you in there, mice?"

She half expected to hear small squeaking noises as she reached and groped, but no sound came from the hidden hollow and her fingers touched no bare mouse body. There was nothing inside except the soft cotton.

"Well, I don't see how *that* got there," thought Cassie and she poked at it again. To her surprise she felt something hard and knobby underneath it, and stretching her arm as far as it would go she managed to pinch at the cotton so she could feel the shape of the thing beneath. It was pointed like a star—and as Cassie moved it between her thumb and finger she felt a sharp prick.

"It's a pin!" she exclaimed. "A star-shaped pin. *Oh!*"

She had found Aunt Emerald's jewelry hidden in the clock, the clock that Mr. Fisher wanted to buy.

At that instant the bell at the front door jangled, and Mr. Bagley, whistling a tune, came into the shop. He stopped dead when he saw Cassie on the chair, his mouth still rounded for the note that did not come.

"Oh, Mr. Bagley!" cried Cassie. "It's here! Aunt Emerald's jewelry's here!"

Mr. Bagley's eyes seemed almost to pop from his head. "What are you talking about?" he said.

"It's here—it's all here—I know it is!" Cassie drew her hand from the opening. In her fingers was a star-shaped pearl pin with cotton clinging to it.

Mr. Bagley leaped forward. "Put it back," he said in a tense voice. "The police won't want it handled. They'll—they'll want it left in the clock just as it is. Give it to me—give me the whole clock, I'll drive straight in to the police station and give it to them."

"No!" said Cassie. "I'm going to give it to Aunt Emerald."

"You mustn't," said Mr. Bagley in his tight, excited voice, "—they wouldn't want you to. They'll want it as quick as they can get it and I'll take it to them."

There was a whiteness around his mouth: he looked strangely changed from the fat amiable Mr.

Bagley whom the whole village liked. What was the matter with him?

And suddenly Cassie knew—it was not Mr. Fisher who had stolen the jewelry and hidden it in the clock, it was Mr. Bagley.

She felt such a thickening of her throat, such a plummeting of her stomach, that she was frozen on the chair. She stared wild-eyed at him. He seemed to loom enormous, like something in a menacing dream, as he made his way toward her around the crowded tables and chairs. He was smiling at her, but his smile was not really a smile. Cassie couldn't stir or speak. Panicked, she thought: I'm alone in the shop with him. There was no Fergus as there had been in the terrifying minutes in the lodge, there was only Aunt Emerald upstairs. He'll take the clock, she thought, he'll take it and run away with it—oh, how can I keep him from getting it?— *what will he do to me?* She felt trapped—small, desperate, helpless.

Mr. Bagley reached the chair where she stood— and at that moment, over the pounding of her heart, came the familiar sound of her father's car stopping

outside and the slam of its door. Cassie's throat loosened and she heard her own voice, high and shrill.

"Dad!" she screamed. "Dad!"

Mr. Bagley spun to face her father as he came running through the door. "She's found the jewelry —she mustn't touch it!—no one must touch it—I'm going to take the whole clock in to the police."

He whirled back toward Cassie. "Give it to me," he said. "Give me the whole clock!" He put his hand roughly on her arm.

Her father was there like a bullet. "Take your hand off her," he shouted.

Mr. Bagley dropped his hand and backed away. There was a clatter on the stairs and Aunt Emerald rushed into the room. "What is it, Cassie?" she cried. "I heard you call—"

"Your jewelry, Aunt Emerald—it's in the clock! Mr. *Bagley* put it there!" Cassie, shaking and half sobbing, held out the pearl pin.

Aunt Emerald stared at it, speechless.

"No, no, Mrs. Blomquist, of course I didn't— you can't believe I did it." Mr. Bagley mopped at his face with a handkerchief. "Let me take it in to the police," he pleaded. "It's the only thing to do."

"No," said Cassie's father grimly. "We're going to look right now. You stay where you are. Get down, Cassie." He reached up his strong hands and helped her down. He patted her shoulder. "You're all right now," he said.

Cassie's legs were trembling. She sat down abruptly on the edge of a chair. Her father lifted the clock from its shelf and set it on a table. He took a knife from his pocket and loosened the screws at the back. Carefully he removed the thin board that covered the lower part of the clock, and Cassie heard Aunt Emerald draw in her breath as they saw what was inside. There were wads of cotton all around the metal wheels and cogs, and glinting among them were the greens and blues and sparkling whites of Aunt Emerald's necklaces and rings, bracelets and earrings and pins. Some of them spilled out onto the table with a little tinkle.

Cassie jumped to her feet. "It *is* there! It *is* there!" she cried.

Aunt Emerald, as though in a daze, picked up a diamond ring and slid it onto her finger. She raised her hand and laid the ring against her cheek while with the other hand she touched, one by one, the bright pieces of jewelry that Cassie's father took out of the clock.

"Cassie, Cassie," she murmured, "you've found it."

In the excitement of discovering the jewelry Cassie had almost forgotten Mr. Bagley. Now she turned and saw that he was edging away from them.

"No!" she yelled. "Don't let him get away!"

She hurled herself after him and grabbed his sleeve. Mr. Bagley jerked his arm away and dashed toward the door. He was almost there when it opened and Corporal Phelps and Trooper Wallace, with Fergus at their heels, stepped into the room. Mr. Bagley tried to fling himself past them, but Trooper Wallace spread his arms, huge and forbidding, and barred his way.

"He stole the jewelry!" Cassie shrieked. "Look —it was all in the clock!"

They looked at the shining heap on the table and at the open clock with its stuffing of cotton and more jewels.

154

"Yeeps!" said Fergus.

Corporal Phelps walked over to the table. He looked pleased. "So that's where it was," he said.

He turned to Mr. Bagley who stood, white-faced, beside Trooper Wallace.

"You're under arrest," said Corporal Phelps. "Take him out to the car, Willie. We'll get a statement from him at headquarters."

Without a word Mr. Bagley, as shriveled as an exploded balloon, went out the door with Trooper Wallace. Aunt Emerald sank down on a chair.

"Mr. Bagley?" she gasped. *"He* did it?"

"I'm sure he did," answered the corporal. "How did you find the jewelry?"

"I found it!" said Cassie. "I noticed that Hansel and Gretel and the witch had moved on and at first I thought the clock was going again but then I saw it wasn't so I climbed up because I thought a mouse had built a nest inside." Her words tumbled out breathlessly. "And when I stuck my hand inside I felt the cotton and then I felt the pin! And at just that minute Mr. Bagley came in and he tried to get the clock—and oh, I was so scared!"

Her father put his arm around her shoulders.

Aunt Emerald said, "Oh, Cassie, darling—!" She reached out and took her hand. "And I was in here most of the morning and I never noticed the figures."

Fergus said proudly, "Cassie's very observing."

Corporal Phelps smiled at her. "Thanks, Cassie. You've saved us a lot of trouble. Here's your earring, Mrs. Blomquist." He handed her the pearl earring that Cassie had found under the lilac bush.

"But how did *that* get outside when all the rest was in the clock?" asked Cassie's father.

"That earring was one of the things that interested us most," said the corporal. "I'll explain about it later."

"You'll come back soon, won't you?" begged Cassie.

Aunt Emerald said, "Could you come back for supper tonight, you and Trooper Wallace? Then you could tell us all about it."

"Why, thanks," said the corporal. "I think we can get off by then, and we'd like to very much."

Fergus, looking eager though slightly embarrassed, went quickly up to Corporal Phelps and whispered something to him. The corporal laughed and nodded. "Okay," he said.

Aunt Emerald followed him to the door. "I'm so glad you can come," she said. "I'm so very grateful to you."

"You don't need to be grateful," said the corporal. "Cassie discovered the jewelry, Adam could have made the arrest—why, you hardly needed us at all." He winked at Cassie and went out the door.

"What did you *say* to him?" Cassie asked Fergus.

"Wait and see," answered Fergus mysteriously.

CHAPTER 11.

THE village buzzed with the news of the jewelry hidden in the clock and of Mr. Bagley's arrest. Cassie's mother was the first to be told. She had been in the cellar and had heard none of the commotion in the antique shop. Cassie met her as she came up the stairs with a jar of jelly in her hand and a cobweb in her hair, and babbled out an incoherent account of what had happened.

Fergus' mother and the Gallups appeared a moment later, followed by Mr. Fisher in dripping wading boots; they had all seen the police car drive off with the wilted Mr. Bagley in it, and in no time at all the news had spread around the village. People flocked to The Rocking Horse to congratulate Aunt Emerald and to praise Cassie. Red Rivers, flaming again, brought his mother in his car; he helped her up the steps and stood beside her holding her arm while she laughed and cried at the same time.

Cassie told her story over and over again, tingling with excitement and remembered terror as she described Mr. Bagley's nightmare approach toward her through the clutter of the antique shop.

A few people found it hard to believe that Mr. Bagley was the criminal. Mr. Fisher kept clicking his tongue and saying, "Why, I *never* thought it was Horace Bagley." But the general reaction was rage against him, almost as much for having deceived them as for the actual theft.

"Just worming his way in," said Cassie's mother angrily. "Being so nice to everyone. *Oh!*"

"And pretending to be so pleased about winning my braided rug," added Clara Gallup. "Why, he didn't care a *thing* about it!"

"A thief under my roof," said Fergus' mother in a shocked voice. "I'll never get over it!"

It was long past their usual lunch time when they sat down to a makeshift meal. It seemed almost impossible that so much had happened in the morning, but the afternoon dragged while they waited for Corporal Phelps and Trooper Wallace to come back. Cassie helped her mother get ready for the supper party and made a large batch of fudge to help pass the time.

Fergus had been invited to join them, but by six o'clock, when the table was set and the biscuits were rising in the oven, he had not yet come over, and Cassie could not understand where he was. She was still bursting to know what he had whispered to Corporal Phelps. She went outside and yelled, *"Fergus!"*

His face appeared in a window of his house, peering around the edge of a curtain. Cassie beckoned wildly and shouted, "Come *on!*" but Fergus, skulking behind the curtain, shook his head. What's the matter with him? thought Cassie—and immediately forgot him as she saw the police car come down the road. She ran to meet it as it drew up in front of the house.

Corporal Phelps, with his pipe in his mouth, was driving, and beside him sat Trooper Wallace in a red and black kilt with a matching length of tartan flung over his shoulder. He got out and stood, solemn and majestic, so Cassie could see him in all his glory. From his waist hung a furry pouch and out of the top of one knee sock stuck the hilt of a small dagger.

Cassie stared at him, in awe and admiration.

Across the road a door banged, and Fergus came bounding toward them. Above his knees his own kilt flapped. He stopped in front of the trooper.

"I wasn't going to wear mine unless you wore yours," he said. "Gee, I wish I had all those things you've got!"

Corporal Phelps laughed. "You look splendid, Fergus," he said. "I gave Willie your message and he was delighted to get dressed up for the occasion. Sorry I didn't have anything to equal it. I thought of wearing my Indian suit, but I didn't think it would compete."

Trooper Wallace ignored him. He said to Fergus, "It's a bonny costume, isn't it, now?"

Fergus' eyes shone. He swallowed and said explosively, "Aye!"

"I brought you something," Wallace told him. He reached into the car and brought out a small book bound in tartan. "You can look up your crest in this."

"Gee!" exclaimed Fergus. *"Thanks!"*

"Come on in now," said Cassie impatiently, "so Mom and Dad and Aunt Emerald can see you." She hopped backward so she could keep her eyes on the gorgeous trooper and on Fergus walking proudly beside him.

Aunt Emerald was wearing as much of her jewelry as she could possibly get on; she glittered like a Christmas tree and her eyes were as bright as her jewels.

Trooper Wallace said admiringly, "You look swell, ma'am."

"My goodness, so do you!" said Aunt Emerald.

They all exclaimed over the magnificence of the trooper's costume and complimented Fergus on how

well he looked in his kilt. Cassie couldn't blame him for strutting a little.

"This is a real mutual admiration society," her father said, "but what I want to know is, did you get a confession from Bagley?"

"Certainly did," answered Corporal Phelps. "He broke down and practically wept it all out—we can tell you the whole story now."

"Oh, but wait," said Cassie's mother. "My mind's on my biscuits and my gravy now, and I don't want to miss anything. Wait till we're eating, please!"

So it was not until they were seated around the table and everyone was served that the corporal began.

"The first thing that made us suspect Bagley," he said, "was when he told us he could see the white hat of the woman in the car. We didn't think he could see the head of the person on the far side of the car at all from his window, so I sat there while Willie went up to his room to find out. And he couldn't."

Cassie remembered the experiment. "Of *course!*

We were so busy looking at you we never saw Trooper Wallace in the window."

"Wasn't there any car at all?" asked her father.

"We didn't think so—particularly as Mrs. Banks had decided by then that it was probably the day before she'd seen it. Well, right after that you found the earring, Cassie," Corporal Phelps went on. "When we got it in and checked it for fingerprints there weren't any."

"Not even *mine?*" said Cassie.

"No. You must have picked it up by the setting and they wouldn't show on that because it's all open-work—filigree, don't they call it?"

Aunt Emerald nodded.

"The queer thing was that the big pearl in the middle had been wiped absolutely clean. Now, if the thief went out the window with all the jewelry and just dropped the earring by mistake, that pearl would still have had Mrs. Blomquist's prints on it and his own glove prints—or at least have been all smudged from handling even if it didn't show up any clear print. Why would he wipe it clean if he was planning to skip with it then and there?"

"He wouldn't have!" cried Cassie. "Of course he wouldn't."

"So it wasn't dropped by accident. Therefore it must have been put there on purpose. And the only reason for that was to make us *think* someone had dropped it as he went out the window and that all the rest of the jewelry was somewhere outside the shop."

"The chief thought all that out," said Trooper Wallace.

"Another odd thing about the earring," continued the corporal, "was where it was found, way under the lilac. It couldn't have rolled there in that tall grass; it would have been right under the window if it had been dropped."

"Why did he put it there then?" asked Fergus.

"I'll tell you about that in a minute," said the corporal. "So we figured that the jewelry hadn't been taken away at all, that it had been hidden in the antique shop by someone who was right here in town, almost certainly Bagley. And just then we got the call on him from the Boston police." He took a bite of fried chicken. "This is delicious, Mrs. Clifford. You carry on, Willie, I'm getting behind on my eating."

Trooper Wallace cleared his throat. "They'd checked on him there and hadn't found any record on him. But they had talked to the superintendent of his apartment, and he had a funny story to tell. He'd had to go into Bagley's rooms a few weeks ago to see about a leak in the water pipe, and there weren't any paints or easel or anything like that there at all. But a few days later he went back to check up on the pipe, and the place was filled with painting stuff and some freshly painted pictures. They looked pretty queer to the superintendent, but he didn't know anything about art. He was surprised, though, that Bagley had taken it up so suddenly."

"You mean he wasn't a painter at all?" said Aunt Emerald.

"You could fool anyone with this crazy modern stuff," said the trooper. "He just wanted to pretend he was so he'd have an excuse to settle in for a while. Another thing he did was to bone up on antiques so he could get friendly with you, Mrs. Blomquist. He told us all this when he confessed."

"But how did he know about her jewelry?" asked Fergus.

"Cassie's article was reprinted in a Boston paper. He happened to read it and planned everything out then."

"It *was?*" exclaimed Cassie.

Corporal Phelps grinned at her. "Sort of tucked away as a filler when there wasn't much news," he said.

Cassie's father looked disgusted. "You mean he planned all the time to steal the jewelry and hide it in the shop in something he knew he could buy?"

"Yes," answered the corporal, "and the clock was just made to order for him. He was quite sure he could get in ahead of Fisher and persuade Mrs. Blomquist to let *him* have it—he'd have gone as high as necessary on the price, believe me!"

Aunt Emerald shuddered and said, *"Oh!"*

"Well," continued the corporal, "Fisher hadn't done anything more about trying to buy the clock when Bagley found his opportunity to steal the jewelry and hide it there. He was on his way to get Mrs. Blomquist to sell it to him when he found Cassie had discovered it. He made a big effort to get away with the clock even then, but he went all to pieces when we arrested him."

"Tell about the earring," said Cassie.

"Oh, yes. You see, he had worn gloves when he broke in and when he gathered up the jewelry, but when he got to wrapping the cotton around it and putting it through that opening in the clock, that was sort of tricky work and the gloves slowed him up. So he took them off—he could get the stuff stowed away quicker without them. And then at the last minute he decided to drop the earring out as a red herring."

"Oh!" Cassie burst in. "And then he remembered that his fingerprints were all over it!"

"You're a real sleuth," said Trooper Wallace.

"Let *him* tell it," said Fergus.

"She's right," the corporal continued. "He did, and he was in a panic. He went out the window and picked up the earring and wiped it all over with his handkerchief. And in his excitement and hurry he threw it farther away than he meant to. That's how it got under the lilac."

They were all silent for a minute. Then Fergus asked, "What'll happen to him?"

"Oh, he'll get five to ten years," replied the corporal. "Plenty of time to think it over."

Aunt Emerald sighed. "I wish I could forget the whole thing," she said. "It's sickening."

Trooper Wallace turned to Fergus. "Why don't you look up the MacDougalls in that book? Read Mrs. Blomquist about your crest. That'll cheer her up."

"Do, Fergus," said Aunt Emerald.

Fergus jumped up. He got the book and riffled through the pages.

"Here's the MacDougalls!" he said excitedly. "Look, there's a picture of the tartan and here's about our crest. Listen! 'An arm in armour embowed fessways, couped, proper—'" he hesitated and went on slowly, "'—holding a cross crosslet fitchy, gules.'" He looked up, completely baffled, at Trooper Wallace.

Aunt Emerald laughed delightedly. "It's marvelous! What does it mean?"

The trooper took the book from Fergus. "It's a

real fancy-sounding one, isn't it?" he said. "Now, let's see. Embowed means bent, and I think fessways means going horizontal. Couped means it's cut off clean, and proper means it's in its natural colors. A cross crosslet—I guess that's just a small cross. Fitchy means it's pointed at the end and gules is red. So—you've got an arm in silver armor holding up a red cross."

He beamed at the admiring faces around him.

"Why, Willie," said Corporal Phelps, "I didn't know you knew about heraldry along with all your other accomplishments."

"It's nothing," said the trooper modestly. "I just looked them up in the library when I was figuring out the Wallace crest."

"Oh, what's yours?" said Cassie.

Trooper Wallace expanded his chest and looked more imposing than ever. " 'A dexter arm vambraced, the hand brandishing a sword, proper.' That means the right arm, in armor."

"Just like mine," said Fergus happily, "except you've got a sword and I've got a cross." He took the book and studied it again. "Yeeps! I've got a war cry! It's in an awful funny language, but it says it means 'Victory or Death!'"

"That's Gaelic," explained Trooper Wallace.

"Victory or Death!" repeated Cassie. "Oh, that's a wonderful one, Fergus."

Fergus looked as proud as a prince.

They were just finishing their cherry pie and Cassie was wishing she had a crest and a war cry when there was a knock at the front door. She ran to open it and was surprised to see Mr. Tobin, the owner of the Shetland ponies. His truck was parked behind the police car.

"The news is all over the Flats," he said after he had been introduced to the officers. "Thought I'd just drop in and congratulate you. I'm real pleased you got your jewelry back, Emerald."

"Oh, thank you," said Aunt Emerald. "So am I!"

"I understand you found it, Cassie," Mr. Tobin went on, "and there you was, just a little girl, all alone in the shop with that crook threatening you."

Cassie relished the description of her dramatic moment. "Oh, it was awful, Mr. Tobin! But Dad came right away, and then Corporal Phelps and Trooper Wallace came and arrested him."

"Still and all," said Mr. Tobin, "I figure that without you finding it he might have got away with it. So you're kind of a local heroine, so to speak, and I've brought you something. A little reward, you might say."

"Brought *me* something?" Cassie exclaimed.

Mr. Tobin crooked his finger at her and smiled slyly. "You come with me," he said, "and see if you like it."

Cassie followed him out the door and everyone else came after them. Mr. Tobin went straight to his truck and let down the tail gate.

There, on a heap of straw, lay the colt, Minute.

"Oh!" gasped Cassie. "It's Minute. Oh, Mr. Tobin, is he for *me?*"

"That's right. I knew you got real attached to him last night and he liked you, too. So I figured I'd just make you a present of him on account of all you went through."

"Oh, Mr. *Tobin!*" said Cassie again. "I never had such a wonderful present in all my whole life!"

She scrambled up into the truck and flopped down on the straw beside the colt. "Oh, Minute," she whispered. "You're mine now." The colt whickered and rubbed his head on her shoulder.

"I'm glad you're pleased," said Mr. Tobin. " 'T ain't much of a reward, though. *You'll* have to buy his feed, Adam." He cackled merrily.

"That's all right," said Cassie's father. "It was nice of you, and I think Cassie deserves him."

"So do I," said Aunt Emerald.

Mr. Tobin lifted Minute out of the truck and Cassie jumped down after him. Everyone patted him and exclaimed over him, and Cassie felt as though she would burst with joy. Fergus might have a crest and a war cry—but *she* had a real live baby Shetland pony!

Corporal Phelps turned to Trooper Wallace. "Willie," he said, "how about giving us some music on the pipes? It would add to the festivity."

The trooper looked unaccountably shy.

"The pipes!" shouted Fergus. "Did you really bring your bagpipes?"

"Well, I put them in the back of the car just in

case," said Wallace. "But you don't really want to hear them, do you?"

"*Yes!*" answered Fergus, and Cassie said, "Oh, please, Trooper Wallace. I've never heard them."

"You can put cotton in your ears if they're too noisy for you," the corporal told her. "I often do."

"Well—" Wallace hesitated. "Are you sure?"

Cassie's father and mother and Aunt Emerald and Mr. Tobin all said, "Yes," enthusiastically. The trooper walked to the car and brought out the pipes. "Maybe you better take the colt away a bit," he said to Cassie. "It might scare him."

Cassie led Minute to the steps of the house and sat down. She put her arm over his neck and held him close to her. Trooper Wallace blew hard into the bag to inflate it, his face getting as red as an apple, and then he took a deep breath and began to play. Minute quivered, pricked his tiny ears forward and tossed up his head. "Don't be scared," said Cassie, stroking him. The colt whiffled softly through his lips and in a moment lay down, reassured, on the grass at her feet.

Cassie had never imagined what the music of the

bagpipes would be or what it would do to her. It was like no sound she had ever heard before, strange and wild. It made shivers go up her back, it made her scalp prickle. It was so sad and wailing she felt like crying, so exciting and quick her feet wanted to dance. She sat on the steps with her hand on Minute's neck and watched the trooper, huge and magnificent in his red and black tartan, as he walked slowly back and forth piping his unearthly notes. Fergus walked close beside him, worshiping. His bare knees were knobby beneath his kilt, but Cassie thought he looked handsomer than she had ever seen him.

Her father came over and sat down beside her. "How do you like it?" he said.

"I *love* it!" said Cassie.

The wild music of the pipes swept and swirled down the road; doors opened and astonished faces looked out. Fergus' father came running from his house, Gramma Banks from hers. Within a few minutes a crowd had collected; they stood gaping at the incredible sight of the kilted trooper and his bagpipes. Gradually feet began to tap and faces to smile.

Gramma Banks put her hands on her hips and broke into an awkward little jig—the ribbons in her hair bobbed and danced with her. Fergus' father seized her around the waist and whirled her in a circle, aprons flapping. Aunt Emerald, bedecked and shining in her jewelry, never stopped smiling; even Mr. Fisher, standing beside her, clapped his hands.

Corporal Phelps lit his pipe and said to Fergus as he marched by, "Pretty good, isn't he?"

"He's *great!*" said Fergus devoutly.

Whenever the trooper stopped, voices begged, "Oh, please play some more!" *"Don't* stop."

So he went on and on while the soft summer dusk crept over the white village, The Rocking Horse, the leafy maple trees. Cassie, with the magic music in her ears, thought about all that had happened since last night. She rubbed Minute's neck and leaned against her father's shoulder.

"We *did* have an adventure, after all, didn't we?" she said.

ABOUT THE ILLUSTRATOR

Harold Berson is a native of Los Angeles, California. He majored in sociology at the University of California, Los Angeles, and upon graduation was employed as a social worker with the Bureau of Public Assistance.

Mr. Berson's illustrations for classics such as *The Emperor and the Nightingale* and *Racketty-Packetty House* received wide acclaim. His artwork has also appeared in *Humpty Dumpty's Magazine, Calling All Girls,* and other periodicals.

With his wife, he spent a year and a half abroad doing watercolors and pen-and-ink sketches of the countryside and people in Morocco, Spain, Italy, Yugoslavia, Greece, and Turkey. Mr. Berson and his wife now live in New York City.